Hell of a THING

LAURAE KNIGHT AND
FAYE KNIGHTLY

HELL OF A THING

For those of us who love the spicy AND the deranged. Within these pages your wildest dreams and most epic nightmares will be showcased in all their sickening glory.
Enjoy!

LAURAE KNIGHT AND FAYE KNIGHTLY

LAURAE KNIGHT AND FAYE KNIGHTLY

CONTENTS

Carnival lights and carnival fun,
when the sun goes down, you'd better run.

CHAPTER 1

The most thrilling experience you will find, we offer base jumping from a height of five hundred meters to—

With a roll of my eyes, I stopped reading. Five hundred meters was nothing compared to the base jumping I'd done in Mexico. Too bad money was tight and I couldn't get back there anytime soon.

Next.

I clicked back through my search results.

Our white water river rafting will—

Will what? Bore me to death.

Next.

Hm, bungee jumping in Vegas could be good. Only, I tripped on the words "controlled descent" and slammed my fist down on the rickety desk I'd found at the side of the building after moving day.

The thing almost collapsed under my fist. Whatever. Hobbies like mine were expensive and who cared if my furniture was garbage? You only live once, right? The money I earned from selling photos I took during my escapades covered this way of life, and I was barely home anyway. With a groan, I leaned back, letting the wheels of my chair scrape across the hardwood floor.

There had to be something to do around this small-town layover I was in until I could move back to the city.

An idea came to me, and I jumped up to grab my phone and dial my friend Tom. He was the most likely to go along with my latest plan. I waited patiently as the phone rang, wondering if he was there, frozen in terror at receiving an actual phone call instead of a text. Sure, I could text, but the excitement was buzzing in my ears, and I wanted to actually talk to him.

Tom's voice clicked onto the line.

"Hey, thanks for calling, but I've got bad news for you. I'm out. Leave a message or, better yet, send me a text." With a long-suffering sigh, I gripped the phone.

"So, I have a new adventure for us this Halloween weekend." My hand shot up as if I was talking to him in person. "Before you say no, hear me out. We rent some gear and go camping up in Yellowstone. They've got cliffs we could dive off of. Maybe we'll tell some ghost stories around the campfire." I paused. "Plus, you owe me for introducing you to Carly." I was just about to further the guilt trip and secure my victory when a ruffling sound at the door to my apartment caught my attention. Squinting, I took the two steps to the door and stared in surprise at what appeared to be a crisp, yellow envelope.

What in the world? The words "You're invited" were printed in bold sweeping pen strokes, the calligraphy clearly done by a professional, and I flipped it over to find a red wax seal with a devil head, complete with large black horns, pressed into it.

Intrigued, I ran a finger over the bumps and ridges cut into the wax. But my hand shot back in surprise when I realized the wax was still somehow warm.

Weird. Carefully opening the envelope, I pulled a piece of paper out and found a centered poem written in the same gorgeous calligraphy.

The Devil's Carnival has come to town.

Don't be frightened, come on down.

Life is such a fickle thing.

A glass of wine,

A bit of fun

Before the bell and you're done.

Come on down this Halloween.

You'll never forget the sights we bring.

The Devil's Carnival? I knew there was a carnival in town, but I had no idea they were doing a Halloween thing. Excitement brewed in my chest, and I grabbed the letter, flipping it over to rub my finger along the now cool wax seal.

With a grin, I gripped the letter in one hand and the envelope and phone in the other, marveling at my good luck.

This was just what I needed.

"Tom, I have something even better for us to do."

A cool breeze whipped through the air, carrying with it the sounds of The Devil's Carnival. Bright lights flickered on the Ferris wheel, drawing my gaze to the left. I took a moment to admire the metal monstrosity looming over the carnival below. At a glance, it appeared perfectly normal, but I knew its secret. Some carriages contained special doors hidden beneath the foot trays that would give way at the push of a button. Whether that would be when it was safely near solid ground or at its zenith, would be up to the operator, and he wasn't known for his mercy.

For the moment, those traps remained secure—the brightly spinning wheel meant to charm and delight. Human voices filled the air with laughter and joy.

But not for long.

The rest of the carnival was equally disarming, with canvas tents painted in deep purples, blues, and blacks shielding the games and food stations below. It was a painfully normal carnival meant to lull the local humans into a false sense of security.

A human child with the unsteady gait of an early walker wandered close to where I hid in the folded back curtain of our fortune teller's tent, and I was forced to step back into the shadows lest the tiny cherub spot me. With curly blonde hair and round cheeks, it stared into the darkness, blowing raspberries until thick drool dribbled down its chubby chin.

It was so sickeningly sweet I wanted to vomit. Thankfully, the creature's mother and father called to it in a tender voice, and it toddled back towards them, leaving me unseen within the shadows.

How I hated having to hide myself, but I was far too strong to have left the body I inhabited as recognizably human. Only the lesser demons who weren't strong enough to influence human flesh were allowed to go out in the day and deal directly with humans. Pathetic weaklings. The best those low-ranked demons could manage were a few stubby horns that were easy to hide under a broad hat and with the advent of coloured contacts, no one noticed their strange eyes. But me? No. There was no hiding my crimson skin or the two onyx horns coming to a proud point high atop my head.

The insult of having to hide was soothed by knowing my time was coming. On Halloween, any deviations from a normal human appearance were met with delight, and I was only too happy to show them what the face of a high-ranked demon looked like. A wicked grin tugged at my lips. I belonged in a cautionary storybook.

Too bad the humans didn't heed those warnings, assuming they were products of imagination meant to thrill. What pathetic beings they were. The truth was right there for them to see. Hell, The Devil, Demons, and all the various creatures hiding in the dark, we roamed the world unchecked. But humans preferred to think of us as fantasy—ignoring the ever-present danger barely concealed by the shadows.

In two days, I'd show them.

CHAPTER 2

"Come on, Tom. Please?" There was a pause on the other end of the line, and I pressed my ear against the phone, trying to make out the muffled argument going on in the background.

"Listen, I'm sorry, but I promised Carly we'd shell out and watch a horror movie tonight. You know, Netflix and Chill, if you get my drift. It is a holiday, you know?"

It wasn't that I didn't understand where he was coming from, or acknowledge that sweet Carly, who loved hugs and Squishmallows, wouldn't be interested in coming to The Devil's Carnival, but I didn't want to go alone.

Which was stupid. This was my night, and from what I could see of the fog rolling out of the entrance gate, this place was going to be amazing. At least my camera could keep me company.

"It's okay, Tom. I get it. Really. Talk to you tomorrow?"

"Yeah, of course." Tom's relief was palpable.

"And Tom?"

"Yeah?"

"Can you please put on an actual horror movie to watch with Carly? None of that Shark-Hurricane or whatever shit she thinks is dark." Tom's laughter on the other end of the line warmed my heart.

"Yeah, I'll put on something good. Have fun."

"You too." I hung up just as a grumpy old woman wearing a maid costume walked up with a cardboard box full of cell phones. She gestured with a wrinkled hand at my device.

"No phones allowed inside."

What? I stared in horror at her uncaring face, looking around me to see if anyone else was shocked at her request, but I only saw amusement on the faces of other people in line.

"Oooh. Scary," the college-aged guy behind me said as he swooped his phone through the air before placing it in the box. Reluctantly, I dropped mine on top of the others with a clunk, looking longingly as my rhinestone studded case slid to the side and mixed with the others until it was half hidden. A thrill chased its way up my spine.

Without my phone, I wouldn't have a way to contact anyone.

I wouldn't have a way to call for help.

Thankfully, she didn't request I take the camera hanging from my neck and add it to the pile. She merely offered it a passing glance before moving down the line.

Even more intrigued by the promise of this carnival, I watched as a man in the ticket booth handed the first person in line a clipboard stacked with paper. He had an enormous, hooked nose which he rubbed nearly constantly, and the glazed look of someone forced to do monotonous work for hours on end. His red and white striped vest reminded me of someone from an old theater ticket booth. It was tight across the chest and seemed like something his employer had forced him to wear.

"Sign and initial. Take it off and pass it back," the ticket booth man shouted loud enough to be heard a few paces back.

Going to an attraction where I had to sign a waiver freeing the carnival and its workers of any wrongdoing was exactly my thing, and I stepped forward eagerly.

The people ahead of me barely looked at the paper before haphazardly scribbling their agreement. It wasn't until the clipboard got to me that I realized why they didn't linger on the details. The murmurs behind me from the hundreds of people still waiting their turn were like hot pokers urging me to go faster. Still, I couldn't help but skim some of the bullet points. Something about waiving the right to hold the carnival accountable for injuries, trauma, or death.

Death? Surely, that had to be for theatrics, right?

I decided I didn't care. This couldn't be any more dangerous than skydiving.

Hastily scribbling my signature, my hand paused at the additional details they requested. My birth date? Blood type? Why the fuck would they need to know that? I opened my mouth to ask a question, but someone from behind me bumped my shoulder, only offering a laugh instead of a light-hearted apology.

Assholes. With a roll of my eyes, I filled in the rest with a steady hand before passing it back to the group behind me. I wondered if they'd give the waiver a second thought. Probably not. One of them mentioned an algebra midterm, and by the ruckus that followed, it seemed unlikely.

They signed the contract, practically fighting over who got it first. One tall guy held it high over a girl's head, taunting her with it like a prize. The girl grabbed for the clipboard, and it came close enough to my face that I had to take a step back. But I'd caught the word dismemberment, and it gave me pause. I wanted to take another look at the contract, but an additional window opened up, and the line moved forward, carrying me along with it. Maybe it was for the best. Dismemberment was probably just part of the whole injury clause, anyway. Places like this always needed to cover their ass.

Stepping forward, the familiar weight of anticipation and worry filled my stomach as I handed the paper to the gruff-looking man behind the plexiglass. Scruff covered his chin, and his cheeks were round and blotchy.

"Contract, invitation, and I.D.," he grumbled.

Fishing it out of the pocket of my bodysuit, I handed the items over, along with the entrance fee of twenty dollars. I fought to get every last coin out of the skintight fabric and dropped the funds with a clatter on the table. Ignoring the attendant's glare as he begrudgingly counted out the money I'd quite literally scrounged and scraped together for tonight's adventure, I drew in a shaky breath, smoothing the flap of my pocket down nervously. My pleather outfit left little to the imagination, but it had been on sale and it was an easy choice for the night. Plus, the fabric stretched well, all things considered. If needed, I could probably run pretty fast. I'd make a fuckton of noise, but I'd be able to do it. Not that I planned to, as the stilettos I wore confirmed. Every fiber in my being was set on sticking this night out.

The attendant barely glanced at my driver's license before shoving it back through the little slot and holding out a hand, gesturing for my arm. Holding my camera safe to my chest with my free hand, I made sure not to bump it as I complied, hoping he didn't tell me pictures weren't allowed. Given the fact the woman didn't say anything, I wasn't too worried. With an eye roll at the camera, he slipped on a black paper bracelet, and I figured pictures were fine. He turned my wrist over. Holding my first finger firmly, he pricked my fingertip with one long, sharp black nail. Hissing, I tried to pull away, but he already flipped it back and pressed a bloody fingerprint to the paper.

"Hey!" I snapped, more from reflex than pain.

"You signed the contract. Shut up and move on," he grumbled.

Ripping my arm away, my elbow ricocheted off the thick plexiglass, and I gasped at the flare of pain. Cradling it against my chest, I couldn't help but stare at him in disbelief as he called the next person forward. The guy cheerfully stepped around me. I was still staring at the back of his shirt when he flinched from his own wound.

Unlike me, he held his finger up like a badge of honor. His friends cheered, encouraging him as they rushed forward to get their own at each window. With a deep breath, a smile tugged at my thin lips as reality set in. This was the real deal.

And so was this carnival.

An energy vibrated through the evening, and anticipation for tonight's events filled me with an excitement that sang in my veins. I tilted my head back to the night sky, closed my eyes and breathed it in, spreading my arms wide. Tonight would be *my* night to shine.

The humans were ready.

Ripe for the picking.

Surveying the booths as I moved through the crowd, I paused when I caught the sight of a ghoul hiding in the shadows cast by tall tents on either side. With a crook of my finger, the thing shuffled forward on mismatched limbs. A wave of disgust washed over me. Ghouls were too weak to take the shape of living humans and took only pieces of the dead, cobbling together the best bits to allow them the flesh they needed to manifest in the human realm. This one had taken the parts of a few different children, fitting incorrect limbs to the body and making it so it could hardly move about. The demon's soul had twisted its shape into something new—a creature requiring living flesh to sustain its existence on the earthly plane.

If I'd had my way, we'd be rid of ghouls altogether. Horrifying to look at, ghouls spoke in stilted language, were easily distracted from their duties, and they stank. I turned away as the scent of rot burned my nose. They might reek, but they were plentiful, and I needed all the workers I could get.

If all went as planned, the souls from tonight would meet with the devil's approval and line the shelves of his personal stores. If not, well, it'd be straight back to Hell and a life of torturing pathetic, squirmy worms broken years ago. It was tedious work to prod those whose minds were too far gone to feel the sting of my blades, but someone needed to do it.

A hand on my hip, I glared down at the ghoul, feeling a sense of satisfaction when its bloodshot eyes lowered, and it hung its lumpy, bald head.

"Yes, Mistress?" Dejected, the ghoul played with a wart on its crooked finger.

"I need everyone out in front tonight, Ghoul—everyone doing their part. We're expecting *him* soon." The creature's eyes widened, and mucus dripped from its thick lips in a steady stream at the mention of our impending visitor.

"R-right away, of course, of course. I will do it, Mistress. I will make you proud." Then it smiled at me in a gesture that must have been meant to instill confidence in its abilities, but I didn't miss the eager shine in its eyes or the gleam of its sharp teeth.

"And no sampling. That must be done carefully and at certain stages in the process to ensure a quality product, and by *professionals*." I scoffed, knowing all he wanted to do was tear into the tender human flesh and suck the marrow from their bones. Uncouth slob. He could wait to get his rations just like the rest of them. "You are to stay near the entrance and bring the fear."

With a dejected nod, the ghoul lumbered off towards the ticket booth where carnival goers were trickling in.

With a satisfied spin that nearly sank my high heel into the muck from last night's rainfall, I turned from the blur of lights to my tent and stepped inside to prepare for the ritual.

Inside the modest tent, crimson candles surrounded the summoning circle where one of my more trusted underlings had inscribed the series of runes required to bring The Devil into the mortal realm. With a snap of my fingers, the flames came to life, unbothered by the wind thanks to the thick canvas I'd insisted on. Tying the flap shut behind me, I strode to the center of the room and knelt in front of the summoning circle.

The Devil had full access to the souls of sinners in Hell, but here, we could offer him more. Innocence, brave. Under the guise of the carnival, we could offer him the very best and truest of humans for his special collection, not just those bitter souls condemned to an eternity of suffering.

I shouldn't have been nervous. I'd been sent here for this—to ensure this group of carefully selected humans believed this place was for their amusement so they would sign their souls away, and yet when the time came to face The Devil, even I couldn't deny the twist of my stomach. With a simple gesture, he could end everything I'd worked for and send me back to Hell.

It was paramount that I impressed him tonight.

My heartbeat quickened as I double-checked the lines carved into the wood panel floor. If there were errors in the runes, I couldn't spot them.

Sweat dripped from my hairline, stinging my eyes as I took a steadying breath, wiping at my brow with the back of my hand.

Better to get this part over with. He'd be more than willing to pull a nail from my finger for every minute I kept him waiting. Without further hesitation, I reached under my skirt, removed the ritual knife from the hidden thigh strap, and closed my eyes. The ancient chant floated from my lips with ease, growing in power and demand with each passing second. Pain rippled from my palm to my fingertips as I wrapped them around the blade, squeezing until the skin parted. Hot blood trickled from my knuckles into the center of the sigil as I offered my essence and waited for his response.

Only a second or two passed before the aura shifted, and I felt the fabric of the human world rip apart to admit him.

"Hello, my King." Curse the way my voice quaked beneath the weight of his presence.

The Devil did not care for cowards.

I was Isra, commander of his legions during the war, and I would keep my back straight in his presence.

Familiar fingers wrapped around my injured hand and drew it closer. A warm, wet tongue traced the cut and encircled two digits, licking up the blood as the wound healed and left behind the sting of his venom. Memories of what he could do with that tongue flooded to me, sparking a warmth between my quivering thighs.

"Summoned me right on time. Good girl." His defined, smooth voice sent shivers down my spine. "Stand."

Keeping my eyes tightly shut, I stood in one fluid motion. I knew better than to look before he allowed it. A demon learned from her mistakes, especially ones that left scars. At least he let me keep my eyes, even if it was because he liked me to watch as he brought out the blades he used to carve patterns in my skin.

"Mmm, you have always been my favorite, Isra." Words that mean very little coming from him. Especially when he took the knife from my other hand. Even as I worked to breathe evenly, my body remained tense.

"What would you say is the best part of this mortal body, hmm?" His breath warmed my ear. "The pleasure? Or the pain?"

I hated how much I loved his games. The thrill and terror that warred within my body. Despite the drawbacks of his presence and the potential of loss, I still found myself looking forward to this meeting. One night spent with him nearly provided more pleasure *and* pain than I could handle.

"Answer me, demon." The tip of the blade pushed my black robe to the side and traced my collarbone to the red sweetheart cut corset beneath.

"Pain *is* pleasure," I stated. If only I could see his reaction. Was my answer what he wanted to hear? A tremble of fear shuddered through my frame, even as a bolt of arousal shot straight to my core.

"Look at me."

Finally, I pried my eyes open to see red skin stretched over a broad chest and firm nipples. Dark purple tones deepened the lines of his abs and hips down to his black fur-covered goat legs.

In an instant, the blade dragged across the soft skin beneath my chin, forcing my head up. "I said *look at me*, little demon."

"I'm sorry, my King," I whispered.

Deliberately, he pressed the tip of the knife against my quickened pulse. Red eyes with thin black pupils searched my expression, which I fought to keep neutral. Very few things scared me, but The Devil holding a blade to my throat was enough to take even my breath away.

I'd seen him dispatch countless demons for seemingly trivial offenses.

Sharp pain rippled through my neck as he pressed more firmly, drawing hot blood that dripped down my chest to the curve of my breasts. His twisted black horns glistened in the candlelight as he tilted his head to trail his forked tongue along the same path, cleaning every drop.

Moving the dagger between my legs, he found the slit in my long black skirt and reached beneath it. At first, I thought he was returning the blade to the holster, but then the distinct sharpness moved up my inner thigh. Casually widening my stance, I gave him access, holding myself completely submissive to his touch. A mix of pleasure and fear swirled in my chest as he carefully traced my clit with the tip of the blade. The chill of the metal felt good against my heat as he carefully worked the ball of flesh. Just as I started to relax into the sensation, a jolt of pain overwhelmed the pleasure as he pierced my soft flesh. The pain brought a sense of excitement to the moment. Biting my lip, I worked through the sensation, but a whimper escaped my throat, and I could feel his irritation in the way his wrist tensed. The Devil could cause the most unbelievable pain or indescribable pleasure, depending on his mood, and his face gave nothing away.

Was he pleased?

Was he angry?

Would it be pleasure or pain today?

Life or death?

He wrapped one strong arm around my waist and pulled me close to his broad chest while the other skillfully flipped the knife. The rough handle pressed against my folds. Moaning, I thrust against it, loving how the lines and ridges of the wood grain increased the pleasure as it moved back and forth.

"My king." Moaning, I looped my arms around his neck to press my body against his. I wore very little, but the bits keeping us apart felt like too much. I wanted to rip them off and let his hot skin burn my tender nipples.

With a slight adjustment to the angle, he slipped the handle inside me, moving it in and out without hesitation. The texture of the woodgrain slid through my slick, leaving me gasping. My legs grew weak as he worked my pussy, dragging the tip of his claw over my clit. My breathing picked up. The world started to spin out of control. I broke, bucking painfully against the handle, past it to the cutting edge beyond as the release screamed through me. Digging my nails into his shoulders, I clung to him as waves of pleasure flowed through me, mixing now with the pain of being cut and making it impossible to stand on my own.

Would my weakness please him or anger him?

"You better not disappoint me tonight, Isra," he said, withdrawing the handle.

I breathed a sigh of relief. He was pleased then.

This encounter had been about pleasure and life.

Tilting his head, his eyes never left mine as he brought the knife to his mouth and drew his long, forked tongue across it to taste my fluids. Then down the blade to clean up the streaks of blood with a wicked curl to his lips. "It would be a shame to have to kill my favorite pet."

My heart slammed into my ribs, both from the excitement of the moment and the anticipation of what was to come. Demons were made from corrupted souls. We are what's left behind once all of humanity had been squeezed out of them. Under The Devil's care, our souls last an eternity. Nothing could truly destroy us, only cast us back to Hell, and force us through the process of reforming on the mortal plane. The Devil, though. He could snuff us out in an instant if he chose, leaving us as... nothing. Gone into the void.

It would be a true death. Anxiety twisted my guts, and I tried to swallow despite my newly parched throat. Yet, I spoke with assurance.

"You won't be disappointed, my king."

Heat trickled up my spine from where The Devil's long black claws rested lightly on my lower back. He maneuvered us through the shadows with ease, lending me some of his power so we could pass between the crowds largely unseen. Every now and again, a set of human eyes would spot us. They would nudge a friend to point us out, but we'd already be around another corner, and lost in the throng of people.

No need for anyone to see The Devil yet.

We called the entrance a funnel for a reason. We wanted the humans to advance happily on their own, like little lambs for slaughter. There were frights, of course, but nothing so alarming as to scare them off and cause a panic.

Not yet, anyway. I grinned as we came to our first stop. The ticket booth where everyone signed their lives away before entering. The Devil remained quiet throughout most of our walk, and I couldn't deny how each passing second of silence made my skin itch. Knowing better than to leave his mind wandering, I cleared my throat and offered my most impressive smile.

"As you can see, most of the attendees are more than eager for the festivities. During the days leading up to tonight, only our mild games were open. We have altered those slightly to set the humans at ease, the only frights being a few odd little prizes and fortunes which never should be told."

"Keep talking." The Devil's command only made the wetness between my thighs increase. Absolute power radiated from him. Tension stitched my muscles together, making my movements stiff and calculated. My body, still amped up from the way he'd made me climax with hardly a touch, ached for more.

Mind consumed with what lay within the fur of his lower half, my voice came out breathy. "At night, we open the more dangerous games. The ones that push people's limits of what they'll encourage and participate in. It all starts here, though, at the gate. Once the contract is signed and sealed with blood, their soul is ours for the taking. Next, we begin the process of flavoring and distilling."

The Devil nodded along, his gaze turning critical as he eyed one of the game fronts where humans popped balloons for a prize. I'd modeled it after a real carnival game, and it looked convincingly benign.

Maybe too convincing.

I needed to do better.

Clearing my throat, I launched into an explanation of the trap doors hidden in the Ferris wheel as we rounded a series of tents. Beyond was the ticket booth, where unsuspecting people were pouring through in a steady stream. Ignorant smiles plastered on their faces, they filtered into the carnival with wide eyes. Many looked around, their expressions changing from curious, to impressed, to horrified.

Now that the last rays of sunlight faded into star dust and darkness, many of my little creatures were creeping out from the crevices and screams of shock and fear began to fill the air. Some spirits from Hell were far too twisted to control a human body—even a dead one. They weren't fit to become ghouls, but with a few ingredients and animal parts, I could craft them something temporary. Many of them were designed after various monsters and nightmarish creatures I'd found in musty, old human libraries. The very creatures of their nightmares. They scuttled across the ground, reaching for legs and hands and whatever parts of the humans their claws could catch. One that couldn't be more than three feet tall, with bony arms and legs, scurried from beneath the curtain of a nearby table game towards two women, who screamed as they turned and ran back to the exit.

"Will they be able to get out?" The Devil asked.

"Yes. Weaklings like that are of no use to you, my King. The flavors we're after are far more refined. There are plenty of others with more cultivated souls. This is why I set up the Carnival this way. The contract, the demons, the games, attractions, rides, everything. Each one is a layer of tests to weed out the weak ones. My purpose here is to find the strongest souls for you. Only the strongest, most worthy souls may enter the final show at the end of the night, where they will be harvested for your stores." Just as I finished my explanation, the frail ghoul who'd been hiding between the tents earlier skittered towards a couple.

"*Holy fuck!*" the woman shouted, jumping behind her massive boyfriend. The man clenched his fist. "Stay back! I *will* kick you across the carnival, you little shit."

Strings of large white light bulbs were strung from tent to tent, allowing just enough light for the ghoul to be seen. Mottled green skin stretched thin over jagged bones, thin enough to see blue veins beneath the surface. Every movement of its mismatched limbs looked painful as it bounced from one bare foot to the other.

Rolling my eyes at his antics, I caught sight of a beautiful young woman standing off to the side, taking pictures with a chunky digital camera. She wore a skintight bodysuit made of a leather I couldn't smell. Fake then, a mockery of the human tendency to skin and wear animals—a tendency I rather admired. The neckline plunged, giving the perfect view of her modest cleavage. Her breasts were smaller, her stomach round, hips wide, and ass large. Fear and excitement were written into the tension of her shoulders. Wetness gathered between my legs as I watched her full lips part in surprise before curling into a smile as she raised the camera to take a picture. Curse the metal contraption for blocking the view of her enticing face. At least the black ears atop her head gave me something to look at.

When the ghoul pushed closer to the burly man, he didn't hesitate to slam the sole of his boot into the bare chest of the weaker creature. With a garbled shriek, it flew back, hitting the pavement as it bounced and rolled across the hard surface. I was thrilled at the sight, turning to the waiting mist demon nestled in my shadow.

"Tag that one for the oak barrels. It will pair well with his boldness and give him the most deliciously rustic bouquet," I whispered. A rush of wind let me know the mist demon had gone to do my bidding. The girlfriend whimpered, drawing my attention back to the couple.

"Careful! I don't want to get kicked out of here."

He wrapped his arm around her, pulling her to his side protectively.

"Nothing says we can't touch them. If he wants to get that close, he can deal with the consequences. Either he's paid enough to take our shit, or he should ask for a raise. Not my problem." With confidence, he turned on his heel, casting a glance over his shoulder as he pulled his reluctant girlfriend towards the Ferris wheel.

Too bad I didn't have time to linger here and enjoy the show. With a sigh, I turned to The Devil, finding him transfixed.

"I like that one," The Devil said with a smile revealing sharp pointed teeth. He sniffed the air, his eyes gleaming as his tongue darted in and out. His eagerness thrilled me, but there was more to see, and hopefully the night would end with him permitting the carnival to continue and The Devil's black-forked tongue flickering against my clit.

I could only hope this carnival would be enough to satiate him. Enough to earn some reward. All I needed to do was find the perfect soul to present to him. One forged through fear and desperation. A shining example of what the circus can provide.

The young cat lady lowered the camera and backed away, unwilling to take her eyes off the scrawny goblin-demon who chased after a couple of boys running in her direction. Apprehensively, she watched it all with a guarded expression.

I grinned. Smart girl. I'd have to watch that one. She could be the perfect addition to our special collection.

Smiling up at The Devil's glowing eyes, I gestured with one arm. "Come, my King. You'll want to see this."

Chapter 3

Astonished, I wandered around each booth, taking in the games. Some looked mostly normal, if not a little strange, like throwing darts at balloons filled with fake blood. Only the consistency of it was something unlike anything I'd seen before—viscous but oozing in a way corn syrup simply wouldn't do. Shelves of various imitation eyeballs stocked the walls behind. Pausing, I took a few pictures, admiring the shine of the lacquer on the wood. The eyeballs were incredibly lifelike. Some even oozed a creamy fluid, despite how vitreous they were. Damn, this place was impressive.

But when I came upon the dunk tank, I started to question the legality of this place. It seemed normal, a plexiglass cylinder with a target in front and three ratty tennis balls the customer could throw at a dinged up metal target. A plump version of the weird goblin thing I'd seen earlier, but with a pig face, sat in the tank on a platform, jeering at the passersby until a guy with a fake mustache and a cowboy hat arrived.

After paying, he stepped up to a line of tape, his arm winding up like I'd seen pitchers do, and he launched the projectile with a steadiness that spoke of some long-ago baseball lesson. He hit his mark. The pig-like creature plunged into the vat with a squeal, and no sooner had he splashed into the liquid than bubbles and steam erupted, as though it were boiling. Words can't describe the gut-wrenching garbled scream that came from that poor thing, its open mouth revealing a pitifully few broken teeth in a sea of gums. I told myself they had to be in costume and acting for the crowd. Except the clear water became a murky maroon, and by the time it found the rope and pulled itself back onto the now flat ledge, their femurs dangled with bits of meat falling off. They flailed in and out of the liquid, screaming as it sloshed over new flesh and were still writhing when two men dressed as decaying clowns begrudgingly moved to assist them.

Many of the onlookers cried out, some covering their mouths or averting their gaze to the scene. A lot, though, including the cowboy himself, pointed and laughed at the pained cries of the mutilated thing. As much as I hated to look, I took a few pictures in the hopes of understanding the trick later, when I had time to properly analyze it. I couldn't understand how they'd created the nauseating smell surrounding the area as the steam wafted over the crowd from the bubbling water. Something like putrid bacon being fried. It made my stomach heave. Quickly, I turned and moved a few buildings away in the hopes of avoiding the toxic fumes.

The effects here were outstanding. Like, blockbuster movie level amazing.

Effects. This place was what I'd been looking for. Maybe it didn't feel like it, but my harness was secure. There was no genuine danger here. Just something safe to make me question reality.

But I couldn't stop the shaking in my legs as they carried me away from the horrors of the dunk tank. I peered around the surrounding tents for an exit. Not because I wanted to leave, but because a little voice in my head demanded to know a way out. Rolling my shoulders, I worked to clear my head.

I was being stupid. I'd just figure out where an exit could be found and go back to enjoying the carnival. Sure, I loved danger and thrills, but there'd always been a harness, a clip, a parachute, some way of knowing I was safe so I could savor the thrill. This felt different without the safety protocols being shown to me. My breath quickened as I pushed my way through the crowd, not finding an end to the games and attractions lining the long corridor of The Devil's Carnival. There had to be a way through, a break in the canvas marking the perimeter, but there wasn't one. I almost walked past the haunted house, but the flickering white lights of their sign caught my attention on the edge of my peripheral—*The Devil's Playground*. It was like they were flickering for me, but, no, that was stupid. Childish. Even as I watched, the pattern of the flickering changed in an intentional wave where it had been erratic before.

What was going on here?

I wanted to continue, but my body wouldn't respond. It was all I could do to stare open-mouthed, long enough that I could taste the sickly-sweet carnival air.

The haunted house appeared to be a converted fun house. The entrance formed in the shape of a clown's mouth. Someone had fucked up its face by bashing in an eye and knocking out a few teeth. Innocuous, really. The haunted house had always been my favorite attraction, and I had fond memories of laughing my way through the jump scares, unphased by the costumes and cheesy soundtracks.

This one, though. People waited at the gate in a thick line. Carnival workers dressed as clowns tormented those waiting. Two of them held butcher knives, their emerald-green jumpsuits splattered with blood. The fake weapon wasn't what made me uneasy, though. Yards away from the back of the line, I froze in place when one of the two men locked eyes with me. What I thought would be some cheap rubber mask seemed real enough to make me second guess everything I knew about latex masks and prosthetics.

Thick black thread held together patchwork skin stretched a little too tight, conjoined like a torn-up piece of artwork on the sides of his mouth. One stitch through each cheek pulled the corners of his mouth up into an unnatural, tight smirk. My instincts urged me to run, but I wouldn't succumb to the fear. Holding my camera firmly, I forced myself to work through the terror and take a few pictures of the clown, who seemed to tilt his head and raise the knife in a sufficient pose for me. Somehow, I'd drifted closer to The Devil's Playground, and I became aware of people lining up behind me.

The patchwork clown watched me with an unwavering gaze, and the unease in my gut grew heavier. I blinked, and he was closer, but I refused to move away.

He turned from me and charged after another group, pausing right before he connected. Amused, their laughter filled the air. Then he turned back to me. One step after the other. As he came closer, I realized how much taller than me he was. With broad shoulders and the outline of large biceps beneath the fabric of his sleeves, he flexed the fingers around the knife. Up close, the knife looked a lot more realistic. Fake coagulated blood stained the part of the metal attached to the hilt. His fingernails were colored with the same substance.

Unwilling to back down, I kept my feet on the pavement as he stopped only a yard away. From here, I could see his pale blue eyes. They would be beautiful if it weren't for the way they examined my face and body like he was a bear, and I a piece of salmon hung out to dry.

"Can I help you?" I asked.

He moved quickly, his knife flashing when he extended his arm to press the tip against my chest. Fake knives didn't flash like that, and I should know. I'd handled a few when I'd worked part time at the theater. The next moment, he pressed a very real, very pointy tip into my throat, dimpling my skin near the jugular.

This time, it wasn't stubborn defiance that kept me in place, though I wished it was. Instead, genuine fear flooded my system with adrenaline.

This man was unhinged, and I was at his mercy.

"What are you doing?" I asked, my voice far weaker than intended.

Without a verbal answer, he slid the knife along my exposed collarbone from one side to the center of my chest. I sucked in a breath and held it, not daring to breathe lest the movement press the blade deeper. He trailed the knife along the curve of the cleavage of my left breast, where it stopped at the strap of my camera resting in the neckline of my catsuit.

"Take it off." It was an order. One spoken by his deep, rough voice, as though his vocal cords were sewn together like the rest of his gruesome face.

"What?" My heart thumped against my chest.

Someone behind me shuffled back a few steps, clearly wanting to avoid the situation. A sobering reminder that even in an area filled with hundreds of people, many wouldn't stop to help if something genuinely bad happened.

But nothing bad would happen to me at this carnival, right? This was all for show. I was beginning to wonder if the risk of *death* on the contract might not have meant *accidental death*. No, no, contract or not, straight up murder was still illegal.

He had to follow the law like everyone else.

I just had to remember that. As scary as this man was and as real as his knife was, he was still a carnival worker, an *employee*, not some monstrosity like he appeared to be. The jagged breaks in his skin must've been drawn on by a talented makeup artist. Or maybe they'd used prosthetics. That seemed more likely, and I found myself studying the gashes for some sign they were latex.

"Take. It. Off," he growled, his patience growing thin. I wasn't sure if he meant the camera or my clothes, but my refusal remained the same.

"No."

His pupils dilated. His brows raised. The stitches in his top eyelids pulled taut, the skin puckering around the coarse thread. It took only a flick of his wrist to cut the strap of the camera, which rested safely in my hands.

Pain, like electricity, pulsed through my shoulder. Glancing down, blood seeped from the paper-thin cut he'd left behind. His other hand grabbed the tattered straps and yanked. In my attempt to hold on, I stumbled forward, nearly bumping into his broad chest.

"Mine. You signed the contract," he stated.

Looking into his eyes once more, I got the distinct impression they really were dead. The brilliant blue sheen on top I'd mistaken as the color of his eyes now reminded me of cataracts. He shouldn't be able to see through the milky film and yet, he stared straight at me and grinned as though pleased I'd noticed. My breath caught, my mind racing.

A bloody thumbprint flashed through my head, and the weight of realization made my shoulders stiffen.

I'd signed the fucking contract. I was at his mercy. Glancing around only confirmed it. Every single carnival-goer nearby who caught sight of my situation either shrank away with fear or, worse, they laughed.

Didn't they realize I was hurt? Didn't they care he held a knife to my gut, even now?

No. Of course not. They probably thought I was in on it—a paid actor. Were some of them paid to laugh? Certainly, but all of them couldn't be. Flushing with embarrassment and anger, I relented and released my precious camera. Maybe he'd be adding it to the cellphones.

Grinning, the wretched clown stepped back and began to whistle, spinning the camera by the straps, his gaze never leaving mine.

Still reeling from the encounter, I decided this place might be too dangerous. Risking my life by jumping out of planes and off cliffs was one thing, but willfully putting my life in the hands of demented carnival workers was another. Not to mention, I wanted to claim my camera before someone else could, if that was an option. The spell from earlier broken, I made to step out of line.

"Next!" the woman at the gate called. When had the line advanced so much? I was near the front, the black of the entrance's mouth steps away. A firm hand gripped my shoulder, shoving me forward. From the corner of my eye, I caught the patchwork face, partially obscured by my camera, as he snapped a picture of me stumbling through the mouth. I barely caught the jagged ridge of one of the clown broken teeth, steadying myself even as the plywood dug into my palm.

People poured around him, waving the credulous sight away as cheesy Halloween attire. They threatened to trample me, forcing my release of the wooden anchor, and shuffled me into the haunted house even as I protested, trying to squeeze through them.

"No, stop, please. I don't want to go in," I called out, but the sound of excited chatter around me drowned out my voice. Once I was past the door, I pressed myself against the wall until the crowd passed, but when I turned to leave, the door swung shut with a deafening bang, and the room filled with a flickering, dim red light. Any attempt to push the door open failed.

The air inside was thick and heavy. Clutching my chest, I struggled to force it into my lungs. A feeble bang on the door yielded no result, and with the haunting image of that hateful clown and his terrifying eyes still in my mind, I knew that even if it did, I was fucked.

My breaths came short and quick, growing more ragged as the panic built. Forcing my eyes shut, I pictured landscape all around. Instead of absolute darkness, I could see green grass and tan fields coming closer as cold air whipped strands of hair across my face with a soothing sting. Somehow, free-falling towards the earth seemed more feasible than inching deeper into this musty building. There was a time, though, on my first jump when I hesitated, just like now, but I never let that fear stop me. The payoff was always worth pushing past my nerves. I just needed to breathe through the panic, just like I did then. There were safety protocols in place here. There had to be. Even if I couldn't see them.

Something tickled my nose. My eyes shot open as quickly as my hand smacked my face, expecting a bug of sorts, only to find my hair as the guilty culprit.

There was a breeze. It didn't feel like it, but there was. There was air here, even if it felt like I was suffocating. I took what should have been a deep breath and choked, curling forward with a cough.

Where was my parachute now?

My clip?

Instead, it was just me and the darkness.

The others didn't look back, not one of them. They were only a few yards ahead now, but I didn't feel the need to catch up to them. High-pitched laughter broke through my panic, and I looked up to see a girl dressed in a nurse costume, jabbing at a skull-shaped candelabra set into the wall. She smiled as she pulled back a finger coated in brown liquid, holding it up to her friend with a triumphant cheer.

That used to be me.

Pumped for the thrill.

Fearless.

Who the hell was I now? I stared down at my trembling hands.

Weak, pathetic, afraid.

No, I was the girl who laughed when others shrieked. This place felt real, every bit of it, but it was all an illusion. It had to be. Clearing my throat, I stood straight, wiping my sweaty palms against the slick material of my jumpsuit. Hoping no one had seen my outburst, I hurried down the hallway after the others. My eyes struggled to adjust to the flickering red light of the candelabras set into wall sconces. Longing for enough light to see properly, I had to make do with the little that was available, running my palms along the walls for safety as I tried to quicken my pace and catch up with the others.

I was going to make it through this house and out the other side, dammit. I would prove to myself that this place wasn't real.

My straps were secure, the parachute tight on my back.

I pressed on.

CHAPTER 4

"You see, my King? Humans always act sophisticated, but whenever put to the test, they will not only let those around them suffer, but laugh in the face of the dying. Many of them are ignorant enough to believe they're immune to the pains of this world. There are a precious few who truly stand up to injustice. It is those souls we are after. Finding them is a challenge, but well worth it. Those are the souls I offer to you, my King. The kind you would not find within the red gates." Closing my eyes, I let out a soft sigh and casually leaned against the wall of the dark room. One of the things I enjoyed about Hell was the closeness I got with human souls.

"Which one do you think will be the best of this batch?" The Devil asked.

A smile tugged at the corners of my lips as I recalled the little kitten, shaking off her fear. "I've always been a cat person..." We'd followed the last group of humans into the attraction and got a delightful view of her pathetic attempt to escape. One little run-in with Claunid, a once proud chaos demon now disguised as a clown, and she lost all the nerve she'd gathered at the ticket booth just a short time ago.

"Something tells me she's going to produce the most exquisite flavor. Humans drawn to this attraction have an earthy quality."

"What's going on? Where's the door?" someone asked. A tall guy wearing a letterman jacket ran his hands over the blank wall as though that would make a door appear. "It has to be here somewhere. There has to be something." My heart clenched as a man wearing a hot dog costume shoved Letterman Jacket away and ran his palms up the wall.

Even at the back of the group, I could see the wall was completely smooth. There were no cracks to feel. No handle outlined.

Steady. I needed to remain calm. A barking laugh escaped me, drawing the attention of a cheerleader on the arm of Letterman Jacket. Her look of annoyance pissed me off. I was allowed to make some fucking noise in a crisis situation. I flipped her off, watching with satisfaction when she rolled her eyes and turned back to the wall in front of them.

"Let's go back. Maybe we went the wrong way somehow." Letterman Jacket was a real thinker. Except there had been no choices. Just a long, winding hallway leading to a blank wall and a solid dead end.

He turned back anyway, pushing his way through the crowd and shoving me so hard I caught a whiff of stale leather

When he was two steps past me, there was an audible click and the sound of a spring being released. A white panel shot out of the wall, gliding across the hallway almost too quick for my eyes to see. It locked into place on the other side with a click turning our section of the hallway into a cramped room. There were a few nervous coughs from the people behind me as they settled into the new smaller space, but my eyes were locked on Letterman Jacket. He stood still as stone. Like he was frozen mid step.

I stared, ice pounding through my veins as I studied his immobile form.

No, he was fine. It was a trick of the haunted house. Another one of this carnival's amazing effects. He probably was just stunned, trying to decide whether he was injured. My arms were heavy and numb, but I was the closest. Somehow, I reached out a trembling hand to touch his shoulder.

"Hey, you okay, buddy?" It was the slightest amount of pressure, the lightest touch, but he crumbled. The half of his body on our side of the panel slid down with a sickeningly wet sound to fall on its side and reveal a perfect cross section of guts and brains quickly obscured by pooling blood.

Someone screamed.

It might have been me.

A warm body collided into my back, and someone was definitely screaming now, a fucking lot of someones. I took a step and slipped on the blood, falling backwards. A combat boot came down on my arm, and I cried out, struggling to rise only to get a knee to the face. Clutching my throbbing nose, I threw myself backward onto Letterman Jacket's still-warm body and found the space I needed to get my feet under me.

Clutching my arm to my chest, I tried to wiggle my fingers and found I could do so. Not broken then. Turning my attention to my surroundings, a sea of panicked faces greeted me. A motor somewhere over our heads whirred to life, and I watched in horror as the ceiling began to slowly lower. The cheerleader shrieked. I couldn't help but feel bad for her.

"It's gonna be okay. It's a trick, somehow." *Because it had to be. None of this could be real.* I assured myself, working to find a confidence I didn't feel. I didn't have time for her, but I couldn't help feeling bad seeing the genuine heartbreak twisting her face. Not bothering to scramble against the smooth wall where a door should be, I used the deadly panel at my back to make my way over to the side.

There had to be something. Anything. The ceiling lowered enough that the hot dog guy had to crouch in his massive costume, his bun nearly folded in half like a squashed hot dog a kid accidentally sat on. My breaths came in quick angry bursts as I struggled to feel along the wall and keep myself away from the others lest I fall and be trampled again.

There had to be something.

Anything.

More people crouched as the wall lowered. I kicked off my stilettos, embracing my natural stature.

Thank fuck I was short. It wasn't always my favorite thing, but just then, I praised whatever higher power had set my height at five foot three.

A groove met my questing fingers, and I paused, peering more closely to find a switch set into the wall. It was nearly flush with the plaster making it impossible to see. With nothing to lose, I pressed it.

With a click, the ceiling stopped its descent and the wall where a door should be slid upward, revealing nothing but darkness beyond. A celebratory chime rang out as if we'd been playing a game and not almost being crushed by the ceiling. People began to file through the exit and relief poured over me like a bucket of cold water, leaving me exhausted. I slouched against the wall. The crowd of party goers continued to push their way through, heedless of the potential danger despite the horrific death of one of their own. Some animal instinct drove them into the pitch darkness—a preference for the unknown over the sure danger of the room with its crushing ceiling and death panel.

Letterman Jacket's body still quivered, his severed nerves struggling to adjust to their death. A sight which couldn't be faked.

This place was not here to thrill and delight us.

It was here to kill us.

Reaching down to find my discarded stilettos on the floor, I held them in my palms with the points facing out. Peering around me carefully, I took a cautious step towards the open wall. When the cheerleader didn't move from the vigil she'd taken up beside Letterman Jacket's body, I doubled back, placed both shoes in one hand, and wrapped my arm through hers. "Get up. He wouldn't want you staying here, right?"

Only after I yanked her to her feet did she shove me off. "Don't touch me!" Sniffling, she stalked towards the door with me on her heels. She might be a bitch, but my conscience was clear. Once through, we parted ways.

"You killed one?" I didn't like the puckering on The Devil's brow. It bespoke of his wrath—the very thing I'd worked so hard to avoid. I had to play this just right.

"Yes, my King. An inferior being and not suitable for your refined palette. One such as him is easily found in any human city, and would be the first at your gates upon his death." Obsidian eyes shot to mine, and I gulped, fear taking my breath as the anger swirled in their depths.

"You dare presume to tell me what will suit my palette," he growled as only he could, a sound that shook my bones and made the room around us tremble. I knew those out in the carnival proper would feel it. The power of his anger was primal and a part of every being. It rippled through us like an earthquake.

Heat radiated off his body as one cloven hoof stepped forward, leaving less than an inch between us. Not just heat, but a searing one. My skin started to bubble as it came close to the furnace of his body. Licking my lips, I fought to keep the pain from my voice.

"Please, my King, the kitten. She will be worth all this trouble. There will be some deaths in the process, but I promise, she—I will please you. I swear it on the crimson gates of Galek themselves."

The Devil reached out to run a black claw across my cheek. The sting of it cutting through the delicate flesh was greater than it should be. His venom took the sensation higher, stinging me even as it cut, but the mention of Galek the destroyer, who'd reinforced the red gates with the bones of Hell's rebels, calmed him.

"She'd better be."

KITTEN

The new room was a tiny box barely large enough to accommodate our group. Like the hallway, the room was entirely white, from the ceiling to the floor. My stomach turned, the surrounding white making it hard to tell which way was up. There was no door that I could see. Every inch of the space was illuminated by bright fluorescents overhead. The moment I crossed the threshold, the panel slid shut behind me.

There was no way out.

Fuck. Another dead end?

A petite blonde wearing an angel costume started to cry, sending her tight ringlets bouncing, and my heart clenched. She looked so lost and alone.

"Hey, don't worry. We'll get out of here," I promised. A tear-stained face with wide blue eyes and rosebud lips looked up at me with hope.

"You think so? That boy, he—" With a shudder, the angel wrapped her arms around herself, shrinking inward.

"Yeah, he died, but we're still kicking. Am I right?" Okay, maybe she didn't need my unfounded enthusiasm right now. Wiping the grin off my face, I awkwardly patted her on the shoulder. So soft, this woman looked like she bathed in buttermilk every night. What had convinced her to come to a carnival such as this? She sniffled pitifully, hugging herself tighter.

"How come you came to The Devil's Carnival? Nothing good on TV?"

Her brows tilted as she pondered a response. "Honestly, my sister would have wanted to. Our parents were really strict, and she loved to irritate them. After she died, they doubled down on me. I always listen to them, but since I moved in with a couple of roommates, I thought I should start experiencing more, you know? Cutting loose. Then I received that invitation, and it was like it spoke directly to me, talking about leaving the past behind and becoming someone new." The girl hunched forward and sniffled.

A chill crept up my spine. I was absolutely certain my invitation had said something entirely different from hers, and if it had, what would it mean?

"Anyway, I guess I thought this would be a fun way to remember my sister and try to find myself." Her voice cracked, tears brimming in her eyes.

Her story tugged at my heartstrings. The tiny angel reminded me of my cousin, Samantha, and the way my aunt and uncle had planned out every moment of her life until she decided to run away and never look back. For all we knew, she was dead on the side of the road somewhere. If only I'd listened to her when she'd said she couldn't take it.

"I'm Mallory, by the way." The angel's soft voice brought my attention back to her bright blue eyes. She held up a hand and gave me a wave that sent the charms on her bracelet tinkling. She huffed out a breath, hugging herself tightly. Something about Mallory made me feel instantly protective of her, like by taking care of her, I could somehow make up for the way I'd failed Sam.

"Well, Mallory, nice to meet you. I'm Lisa."

"*Nice to meet you?* Are those really the words you're choosing right now?" Her face pinched.

I laughed humorlessly. She was right, there was nothing "nice" about this place. "Perhaps not the best word choice, but hey, I appreciate your company. I think it's pretty *nice*."

The phantom of a smile graced her full lips. "Earlier, even surrounded by everyone as we are, I felt incredibly alone. That probably sounds ridiculous, but anyway, talking to you does make me feel better."

"It's not ridiculous. I get what you mean." The camera-clown incident flashed in my mind. Did he still have it? Was he taking pictures as he scared others outside? Pushing the oddly violating thought from my mind, I said, "Listen, Mallory, it's going to be okay. There's got to be a way out. This is a carnival after all, and the carnies need to be able to move around. There are probably passages or something we can use to escape."

That brought a tentative smile to Mallory's pinched face, and I looked around, trying to make good on my promise. Maybe there was another hidden switch in the wall. With a confidence-inspiring smile at Mallory, I squeezed my way through the group and began sliding my hands along the smooth plaster.

I'd just reached the center of the room when a rumbling nearly shook me off my feet. Only the tight press of warm bodies at my back and the wall prevented me from falling. What I'd thought of as a wall on the other side of the space rose into the air, revealing a dark cavern behind. Peering into the darkness, I strained to see what lay within. Was this the next exit? Maybe, but something about it didn't feel right.

The darkness came to life, and I gasped as movement within the shadows caught my eye. Struggling my way through the panicked crowd back to Mallory, I took her hand and squeezed. She pressed closer. Not hard to do given how the crowd leaned away collectively.

"Just stay with me." A clacking sound came from within the darkness and a skittering of legs across the tile made me shutter, but I couldn't see what it was no matter how I strained my eyes. My limbs were heavy and numb, but I had no fear of being trampled here. No one could move enough to do so. Instead, we were tightly packed, and at the mercy of whatever creature lay in the darkness.

I struggled to lift a stiletto up, but with the door now revealing a new threat, everyone was screaming and surging backwards into Mallory and me.

The press of bodies made it hard to breathe. Around me, I caught glimpses of wide panicky eyes, like a herd of farm animals realizing they were being led to the slaughter.

I may have been short, but I had enough substance to protect me from the jostling, while Mallory was starting to sink beneath the crowd.

Tugging at her hand, I pulled her towards me, wrapping my arms protectively around her and trying to keep the press of the people off.

A roar echoed around us as the thing in the shadows emerged.

The monster that appeared was at least ten feet long, its legs scraping the floor as it fought to bring its bulbous body closer to us, its prey. Rearing back, the creature revealed a long slit down its abdomen surrounded by sharp gnashing teeth.

A fucking centipede? The creature's legs stretched forward and grabbed onto the thick padding of Hot Dog's bun, pulling the helpless man towards its middle.

"Help! Oh God. *Please*, someone, help!"

There was no way I could make it through the crowd in time to be of any assistance, but the logical thought didn't keep me from trying. The centipede pulled him into itself, setting down on its legs to bury him beneath its rotund body. Blood squirted out the sides of the beast, and the man's pitiful screams cut through the panicked shouts of all the rest.

The body of the beast undulated in a pleasant rhythm as it enjoyed its meal. Tears slid down my cheeks unchecked as I continued to try to fight my way forward, failing even as the man's screams grew fainter.

Once they stopped, I was sure the beast would rear back again and descend on a new victim, instead it turned from us and moved back into its cavern, becoming one with the darkness and leaving behind only a smear of red in its wake.

A cheerful chime rang out as a panel shot upwards beside us, leading us to our next nightmare.

CHAPTER 5

Sweat trickled down my spine, making the pleather chafe as I crawled through the sweltering building. Each room seemed hotter than the last. After so many twists and turns, and up a set of winding stairs, I couldn't imagine still even being within the vicinity of the carnival. Time became irrelevant as we moved, entering room after room that couldn't possibly be supported by the mid-sized structure we'd seen outside.

How could this be real? I kept waiting for someone to open a secret door and flip on a hidden light switch. For a perfectly normal person to appear and laugh off the whole thing. They'd tell me this was a well-done haunted house, pat me on the back, and send me home. But as much as I tried to will it into reality, nothing of the sort happened, and I couldn't afford to be lost to despair. Not when I had Mallory to think of. She was a sweet kid and focusing on her helped me forget the sheer terror of our situation.

How could this place exist? How could they do this to people?

You signed the contract.

My heart clenched.

The horror of the place overwhelmed me, and I couldn't help the panicked sob that escaped from my throat, though I coughed to hide it when Mallory looked over with a puckered brow.

How could I be so stupid? Signing my life away like it was nothing. Thinking it was a joke. Convinced something bad could never happen to me. Foolishly believing these people—no, these *monsters*—would never cross that line.

They thrived on the pain and terror they caused.

Mallory took my hand, her grip firm, but her fingers ice cold. She tugged me forward, and I forced myself to stumble along behind her.

Inside the newest room, a stage was set. Severed limbs hung from chained hooks attached to the ceiling. Blood dripped from the appendages collecting beneath them in small pools. In the center was a raised stage with a man strapped to a metal surgical table. He writhed, turning begging eyes on our group, but he couldn't escape the metal restraints holding him. A massive creature with great horns and the muscular legs of an ostrich stepped forward through a pair of red velvet curtains, extending a long black claw towards the helpless man. I clutched a stiletto in my shaking palm and moved to intervene, but some unseen force prevented me. It was as though I stood watching the nightmare unfold behind a pane of glass, but no glass existed. Instead, the air was solid. Mallory clutched my arm and hid her face in my shoulder. With tears in my eyes, I patted her gossamer hair and forced myself to witness the scene unfold. I couldn't help the man, but at least I wouldn't turn away from his pain.

The captive's eyes bulged when the monster sank a sharp black nail into his shuddering abdomen. The beast made a few long cuts before pinching the edge of skin and ripping it upward to remove a chunk. It held the section up to the audience like a prize before tucking the piece of flesh into its oversized mouth. With each slice of the monster's sharp nail down his limbs, with each pull of skin from his body, the man's screams pierced my ears. Naked and writhing on the table, he begged for death.

"Please. Make it stop. Help me! Someone! Anyone!" His garbled voice would live in my nightmares for the rest of my life. Each time it echoed through my mind, another piece of my heart broke. It was only when the man stopped screaming and lay still that a wall to our left slid open. The monster who had flayed him looked up at us with pits of darkness where eyes should be, but I felt its gaze boring into me. Mallory whimpered, and I squeezed her hand, trying to offer a measure of comfort I didn't feel. Wearing a smile made up of pointed teeth, the monster held up a bloodied hand and gestured to the new doorway.

Spiderwebs covered every inch of the room in a thick layer, and millions of spiders of various sizes and types scurried over every surface. The walls were lined with glass coffins set upright, each one filled with a body at some stage of decomposition. The husks of the older ones' skin, deflated and lacking moisture, reminded me of Egyptian mummies.

There must be a switch somewhere, just like the room with the falling ceiling, but this room was twice the size, and I'd have to feel for it. I hoped whatever *thing* made these webs stayed away long enough for me to find it.

It seemed like in every room we had to work to find the way out, or pay a bloody price.

"Do you think we'll ever get to go swimming at the beach again?" Mallory's question surprised me, and I turned my attention to her, trying to keep an eye on the spiderwebs around us at the same time. "Swimming. You know." Mallory mimed a few strokes in the air. "I just. I was realizing if we don't get out of here, we'll never get to do it again."

It was a strange thing to fixate on, but she wasn't wrong, and I didn't have any words of comfort to offer. When we'd first realized the true nature of this place, I'd thought there must be a way to beat it, but each room seemed more horrifying than the last.

"Yeah, I guess. But I hate water, so I'm not exactly with you on that one."

Mallory chuckled behind her hand, setting off her charm bracelet to tinkling.

"Is that why you have so many beach charms on that thing?"

Surprised, Mallory peered down at the mermaids and seashells on her bracelet. "The beach is where I feel safe," she said somewhat defensively, holding her wrist to her chest.

With a smile, I patted her hand. "Well, let's get you back there, then."

Her face brightened, and a warmth spread through my chest at the sight. I would get this kid out. I hadn't been able to save Sam, but I could make sure Mallory was okay. It was a purpose that gave me the strength to smile and move to the wall like I was redecorating my sitting room instead of searching for a hidden switch that could mean our life or death.

The others huddled in the middle, staying clear of the walls like they were dangerous, and maybe they were. Nothing in this place was as it seemed, but if somebody didn't try to do something, the room would demand another death to release us, and I wouldn't let that happen.

"*This* room is a critical part of my method. The fear is building now that they've met a few of our...performers." Pride tinged my words, and I stood up a little straighter as I thought of how well everyone was doing tonight. "Now we'll give the humans some time to settle into their new space, to *acclimatize* and understand just how doomed they are, and then one of my personal creations will make her appearance."

I grinned at the confusion in The Devil's eyes. Most creatures existed within Hell in one form or another, but few were created new. My centipede had raised an eyebrow, but it was still a creature of Hell-made flesh. My creation would be the one to wow The Devil. It had been a tedious process to infuse the soul of a ghoul into the body of a tarantula, but the outcome had been worth it, and my girl would not disappoint.

After the costumed humans were relaxed enough to start leaning against the walls, a figure scurried out from the shadows in the corner, an area the lights were designed to not quite reach. She dropped down with an audible thud, and the group fell silent as they struggled to see what approached them in the flashing strobes.

Above the whimpers of fear and regret, distinct rhythmic thumps neared them. All the while, the silhouette of my girl became clearer. I watched with pride as Calamity descended from the ceiling, lowering her cephalothorax and grinning with the humanoid face of a ghoul but with the protruding pincers of an arachnid dimpling the rotting flesh of her cheeks. I suppose it was a face only a mother could love.

Smirking, I watched as Kitten stepped in front of her little friend protectively.

"Do you see the kitten, my King? Her determination to continue despite the trepidations is doing something for me. You see, most humans are bolstered by ignorance and a false sense of indestructibility. The most layered flavors come from humans like her. Ones who identify the dangers and understand their fragile mortality, but push the limits despite the trepidations. I don't doubt she is going to lead to something unique for you to taste." I shivered with anticipation.

Calamity stood for a moment, her pincers tapping together as her bulbous black eyes scanned each potential meal, searching for the one I'd had tagged only a short time ago. She, like all my *employees,* knew to follow my instructions with absolute precision. When she found the mark, she didn't hesitate.

A grin stretched across my face as I watched her work.

Good girl.

KITTEN

The architect of the webs was worse than any nightmare I could have dreamt, and I had to fight to keep myself standing. Mallory winced in pain, and I loosened my grip on her arm, unable to utter an apology for hurting her.

Wicked red eyes scanned us, and no one moved. I could almost hear all of us thinking a single shared thought.

Not me. Please, please, not me. Despite my reservations, I inched in front of Mallory, hoping to make her feel a little safer than the rest of us. With a screech loud enough to force a hand over my ear, the spider-thing shot forward, pivoting around me to wrap itself around Mallory's body and sink its pincers into her neck.

Her scream broke the monster's spell, and I renewed my grip on her arm, grabbing the stiletto I'd hooked onto my belt and stabbing at the sea of brown limbs covering Mallory.

"You can't have her! No!"

The thing retracted its pincers from Mallory's neck and turned to me, the red of its eyes glowing like two coals even the strobes couldn't disrupt.

I'd thought the terrible shriek it made was the worst sound I would ever hear, but it paled in comparison to the thing's horrific laughter—the sound of pure joy as it reveled in its malevolent intent. Then its head ducked down, driving its pincers deeper, and Mallory moaned as if she didn't have the strength to do more. I watched it tear into the flesh of her neck, its eyes on me, the sounds of it eating only broken by that horrible violent laughter.

But I still had a grip on Mallory's arm, and I pulled her towards me, refusing to abandon her. A tail like a scorpion shot around from its back and lazily sliced through Mallory's arm at the elbow, leaving me holding her severed hand.

With an all-too-human grin, the spider pulled her limp form back up to the ceiling and disappeared into the shadows, the sounds of it greedily slurping and the crunch of bones pounding in my ears.

Those sounds were sweet Mallory being consumed.

I was supposed to save her.

She was supposed to swim again.

My mouth opened in horror. I came back to myself at the tinkling sound of Mallory's charm bracelet, still attached to the dead wrist I held in my hand and set off by the uncontrollable shaking of my limbs.

With a roar, The Devil wrapped his large hand around my throat and lifted, slamming me against the wall with a crack. My head spun, and I saw stars as I fought to remain conscious.

"I accept that some sacrifices need to be made, but how dare you take an innocent such as she from me." There was a dangerous edge to his booming voice, and I fought to keep my hands at my sides instead of clawing at him as I quickly ran out of air. "Well, Isra, what do you have to say for yourself?" As if realizing I wasn't able to speak with him squeezing my windpipe, The Devil eased the pressure, allowing me to gasp in a quick breath of air.

"It is all for the kitten, my King. This sacrifice was necessary—"

He cut me off with a growl. "She was so pure I could smell her from across the room." The heat of his body increased, his eyes becoming a living flame, and I turned my head as it scorched me. "A rare one, and she was mine. Do you dare take from your king now, Isra?"

Attempting to swallow around his grip on my throat and failing, I chose my next words carefully.

"Yes, and an innocent's death was necessary to break the kitten. That child was pure, sure, but there are a few others like her here tonight. A young girl who came to the carnival as an act of rebellion after her sister's death. She and Kitten may have only known each other a short time, but they bonded well, and that made her special. Kitten will be devastated knowing she couldn't save her. The girl's death will be worth this trouble, my liege. I swear it."

His hand didn't loosen from around my neck, but the fire in his eyes died down to burning embers and he tsked. "Mmm, so you keep saying, and I will give you this chance to prove yourself. But first" —The Devil grinned, his black lips curling up, his eyes glinting cruelly—"you've overstepped Isra, and a punishment must be paid."

A bolt of icy fear stabbed through my middle as I ran through the possibilities.

Was it to be hot pokers? Waterboarding? Perhaps he would stretch me until my joints popped.

The Devil's smile widened as he released me from where I was pinned to the wall and spoke one word.

"Come."

Head bowed, he grasped my hand and pulled me to the wall, fading through it to come out the other side and into the torture room where our group had watched a carnival goer being flayed.

The corpse left behind in the flaying room had already been removed and likely given to the ghouls as part of their daily rations, leaving behind a blood-soaked table in a room full of dismembered limbs hanging on hooks. Without looking back at me, The Devil reached up and slid a large man's arm from its spike. The limb came loose with a wet sound that reminded me we'd just taken these bodies apart before the carnival began, hanging them in here for an extra boost of fear. Their real purpose was to provide a selection for new demons looking for dead parts to stitch together into the form of a ghoul, but the humans didn't know that.

The arm The Devil had selected would've made a fine piece for any ghoul. Belonging to a massive man with thick forearms, it had been cut at the elbow joint, allowing for a separate section of bicep and shoulder. The more difficult a human was to detain, the more expensive the piece, and this one would've put up quite the fight. Yes, it was an expensive piece, and almost certainly lost now to The Devil's nefarious purpose. Turning to me with a smile, he covered the hand with his, closing the fingers into a fist without looking down.

"Table." The Devil pointed at the blood-soaked mess, and I couldn't help but feel a thrill as I passed through the magic barrier to ascend the stage and climb the surgical table. The cold metal prickled my skin as I lay across it. "Are you ready to take your punishment, Isra?" There was an excited edge to his tone that sent a bolt of arousal to my core. Whimpering, I spread my legs. By the way he spoke, there would be an element of pleasure to my punishment, and my body responded to the promise of release, giving way before his power like a tree before a hurricane.

Setting the hand down between my feet, he moved to one of my wrists, strapping it to the table with black leather. Watching his fingers work the leather with ease tightened my core. The sight was enough to have me squirming. He walked around the table, strapping my other arm with the same precision.

After returning to my feet, he picked up the arm and adjusted the fingers. The first and middle fingers were extended with the rest curled. Letting my knees fall apart, my breathing quickened as I anticipated what was to come.

Would it be pleasure or pain today? This was a punishment, so it must be pain, but the Devil was known to sprinkle in bits of ecstasy. Gripping one of my thighs, he pushed it roughly up, getting full access to my entrance. Slick and open, he used the severed arm and pushed the two rigid fingers into my pussy. What I wanted was the heat of The Devil's skin. What I got was ice-cold rigor mortis. Once my fluids covered the appendage, he withdrew it and adjusted the angle.

Squealing, I realized what he intended, and I tensed at the pressure of him pushing the two fingers deep into my ass, pausing only a moment to circle the fingers and stretch the hole. Trembling with every thrust, I pulled at the straps holding me, wishing I had something to hold. Without that, I dug my nails into my palms, hissing at the pain as he pulled the hand out and pressed it against my inner thigh, using my leg to close the fingers into a fist once more. The chill of the corpse eased the burn of the stretched skin. Something I grew thankful for as he forced each knuckle in.

Tensing would only make it hurt worse as he forced the hand in. Through gasping breaths, I consciously kept my muscles relaxed. A task that grew harder with every second ticking by as the arm worked past each ring of muscle until it was fully seated.

The Devil smiled triumphantly. "I knew you could take it."

I couldn't look away from him. His glowing red eyes narrowed as he pushed my leg higher, spreading my cheeks more to get a better view of his work. Tears blurred my vision, and I cursed them for obstructing my view of his face. His hand snaked around my front, the rough pad of his thumb finding my clit, mixing the searing pain with pleasure long enough to bring me near the stars. Then he stopped, withdrawing before I could fly among them. Blinking back tears, I moaned, my head rolling from side to side. This was all he would give me of himself, but in my mind, it was he who fucked me, not the severed arm of some nameless human.

I wanted to talk but could only manage small gasps of breath as he twisted the fist back and forth, heedless of the rhythm he knew I needed. Deeper, he pushed, forcing my ass to take every inch of the muscular forearm I'd admired.

The pleasure shifted to pain and frustration as he continued to work me to the edge of release before pulling the appendage out suddenly, leaving my muscles clenching painfully onto nothing. It was then I realized what the true punishment would be. He wasn't going to fuck me himself, nor would he allow me to climax. By the end of this interaction, I'd be a weeping mess, my body screaming for a release it wouldn't find. At least my juices were trickling down to the arm he held inside me. Soon, The Devil's fingers would be covered in my fluids whether he touched me himself or not. That thought nearly brought me to the brink, but seeming to sense it, he paused. A whimper escaped me, and I bit down hard on my lip. Refusing to beg, although I wanted to desperately.

The Devil licked his lips and forced the arm back in. He grinned, entertained by the sight of my hips bucking helplessly against the appendage. Seeing his satisfaction only turned me on more. He worked my ass until the pain that sparked each time he drew the arm out a few inches and pushed back in was nearly unbearable in its intensity. I tried to time his rhythm, to be ready for the next shock, but he changed the speed and angle relentlessly. It was impossible to prepare. I was at his mercy as I writhed on the cursed table, the leather straps cutting into my wrists.

At some point, The Devil picked up speed, moving in and out of my ass fast enough that I was gasping for breath as the screams tore from my throat. All I could do was scream. Words didn't exist anymore. My muscles tightened against his hold, my toes curled, my legs tried to close, to stop the invasion. Every fiber of my being coiled tighter as he continued mercilessly, his laughter teasing my ears as my eyes closed. Only the feel of his thumb on my clit as he worked my most sensitive hole mattered. I focused on each stroke.

Pleasure and pain blurred together.

"Look at me *now*, Isra." His growl startled me. I pried my eyes open to find him looking directly into them. My breath caught. My cheeks flushed. All I wanted was for him to look at me with praise, but only disgust twisted his features.

I didn't expect the abrupt end, but it came with a soft chuckle from him. All at once, he withdrew the arm and took a step back, letting my leg fall off the table to dangle freely. Whimpering, I felt hollow and open. My muscles squeezed, protesting painfully when they found nothing but air. What had once brought pain was now sorely missed. It was all I could get from the Devil, and a good demon took what scraps her master deigned to give her.

The Devil's red cock stood proudly erect, and I longed to catch the drip I could see forming on the tip, but I knew I hadn't earned such a reward. One did not touch The Devil without his permission.

With a satisfied hum, he unstrapped one of my hands and then the next, but they were too heavy to move at the moment. Even if I wanted to wipe the drool from my chin, I didn't have the strength to do so.

"Clean yourself up. I'll meet you in the big top. I expect a better show there. If not, this desperate, unfulfilled ache in your loins will be the last thing you'll ever feel."

"Yes, my King," I whispered, my voice hoarse.

CHAPTER 6

The Devil's Carnival wasn't a place that allowed the time and space needed for grief. Already, everyone had filed through the next door until only I lingered.

Until only I remembered Mallory. I understood, now, why the cheerleader had been reluctant to leave her companion.

At first, I'd waited with a stiletto in hand, sure the spider would come back, and I'd be ready for it. To do, what? I didn't know. To avenge the girl who reminded me so much of my lost cousin? The girl I'd promised to save. The monster never returned. The sounds of Mallory being consumed ended, and the room was bathed in a terrible quiet.

Tears dripping down my face, I sat on the ground next to Mallory's severed hand and undid the clasp on her bracelet. My vision was so blurry it was hard to work, but I needed to take something of her with me. To know that she had existed, and I, at least, would remember her.

A fresh wave of tears spilled down my cheeks, and a sob shook my middle.

I hadn't been able to save her.

I'd failed.

There was nothing to do about it but to stand up and move on.

Hugging myself for comfort, I stood and peered into the dark. I pulled the charm bracelet out and rubbed a pink starfish charm that was quickly obscured as tears filled my vision.

"I'm sorry, Mallory. Rest now. I'll return this to your parents for you, sweet girl." Sobs choked my words, but if I wanted to make good on my promise, I couldn't afford to be a blubbering mess.

My back to the darkness, I walked forward and moved through the entryway into the next space. As though waiting for me, the door slid shut the moment I entered. The long, thin hallway forced us to stand shoulder-to-shoulder in groups of four. The result was a line leaving us vulnerable on both sides. Not one person stepped towards the visible door at the end of the hall.

There had to be a catch. But I could see the door in front of us. It was so close. Just a short jog down the hallway and we'd be onto the next.

Only none of these rooms had been that easy. Someone in front started to shuffle forward, and I couldn't help but keep my head on a swivel. Trying to check in all directions at once. Waiting for whatever horror this room would spring on us.

All at once, the lights went out, and darkness took my vision. Blind within the hall, I reached out for anything, and my hands fell on the softness of someone's sweater. I had no idea who I clung to, but they were warm and human, and that was good enough for me. We moved slowly forward as a unit, but a scream sounded behind and to my left, followed by a rush of air and the gurgling of blood filling the victim's lungs.

Heart pounding, I moved forward on numb legs, trying to ignore the noises as more of us were taken. I'd made it to a more central spot in the group, trusting to the wall of bodies on either side to keep me safe. But a blast of air and a quick squeak told me this thing wasn't done. Every room had demanded one death before a way out was revealed.

This room demanded more.

My heart hammered in my chest when a space opened beside me. A claw grazed along my arm when the person standing there was jerked away. The panic forced me to press harder against the mass of people in front of me, wanting to sprint, puke, anything except stand here unable to move quickly as death came for us.

"It's time for some entertainment." A jovial voice I instantly hated came through an intercom system I couldn't see. Jaunty carnival music accompanied it. Something about the cheerful contradiction to our life-threatening surroundings made this all that much worse. All I could imagine was a blood-covered clown with a stitched up face resembling the one who'd taken my camera laughing as he watched us.

The sweater I clung to trembled.

"We're gonna make it through this," I whispered to them. "We'll just do what he says. We have to be almost through. I just know it. We'll be at the end of it soon." I was rambling and talking to no one specifically, but I tried to take comfort in my own words.

I could only rely on the shuffling sounds of feet to let me know there were a few of us left. A fact proven when bright lights flicked on without warning. Comfort came in knowing there were others. Even if I couldn't trust them with my life, at least we didn't have to die alone. Spots filled my vision, and when I could see, I realized just how thinned out our group had become. Pausing, I listened for any sound of life from behind us. Surely they weren't all dead? But they were, and I didn't dare look back to see the white hallway stained red with blood and gore. We'd reached the end of the corridor and faced an open door. There was only one way to go, and it was forward.

"Hey, can you let go of me now?" Honey-brown eyes filled with annoyance met mine. I unclenched the fisted fabric and let the girl I held take a step forward. I had no idea what her costume was, but her long blonde hair was tied up in pigtails and the pink fuzzy sweater she wore was at odds with the thick dark eyeliner circling her hazel eyes.

Funny how I still noticed these things when everything around me felt unreal. I'd just survived a fucking cull, but this woman's bad makeup stood out. Probably smeared from crying like the rest of us.

We moved closer together, huddling in a tight group as we looked around the new room, though I tried to avoid bumping into the fuzzy pink sweater. At best, she'd be pissed. At worst, we might have a genuine conversation, and after Mallory's death, I was done getting to know these people.

Not when any of us could be next.

The new room was dim, with white walls just like all the ones we'd passed through. Dirt, grime, blood and gore splash in contrast to the stark white. Metal hooks piercing legs and arms dangled from the ceiling, looking like baited fishing lines for an enormous fish. They didn't look cleanly cut, like the ones from the last room with limbs. Jagged uneven flesh protruded from the ends, as though they'd been torn off the body. These didn't look as new, either. The entire room stunk of decay and sweat. Worse than anything I'd smelled previously. At least outside, with the putrid bacon, I could move away. This was enough to make my head spin.

My stomach churned, both at the assault on my senses, and the thought of the pain these unfortunate bastards suffered.

"There are two doors in front of you," chirped the familiar voice from an unseen speaker.

Damn, I hated that endlessly cheerful tone. Wanted to find the owner of that voice and pummel them into dust. On cue, some hooked parts swished noisily to the side, revealing the doors they'd mentioned. In bloody scribbles, the door on the left read *Yours* and the one on the right read *Mine*. A shiver ran through me as I noticed the care they took to apply extra blood and really emphasize the word *mine*.

"One leads out. The other leads to me. In order for the exit to unlock, I need a sacrifice. One of you must come to me while the rest are free to go. You have ten minutes to decide."

How could such an invitation sound convivial and foreboding at the same time?

"You can't ask us to do that!" I shouted, my voice carrying over the panicked murmurs that began.

Tinny laughter filled the room, hurting my ears.

"*You signed the contract.*"

"What if we refuse?" I called out, clenching my fists. We'd been playing their sick game. Going from room-to-room. Encountering one trauma after the other. Regret wasn't a strong enough word to describe how badly I wanted to take back my choice to come tonight. Part of me, though, felt grateful I didn't convince any friends to come with me. I couldn't fathom the guilt of putting Tom through this all because I thought I loved horror and monsters.

"If you refuse, the door will not open. Another group will come soon, and I'm certain they would be more than happy to pick one of you to be my plaything." Another maniacal laugh followed.

Members of the group looked at me, their faces twisted with uncertainty. The young man with a mop of brown hair who'd looked excited when the room lit up now appeared appalled. Next to him, a woman with jet black hair and mascara running down her cheeks shook her head. "I don't want to die in here like the others." There were unspoken words in the girl's statement, and I felt a chill run up my spine. Like she'd do anything to make sure *she* didn't die here. I surveyed the room, hoping to see the same shock I felt at such a horrifying idea, but I didn't find it. Instead, a sea of grim agreement met my gaze.

Shit.

"Don't you people understand what this place is?" *And what was this place?* I wracked my mind. The demons, the torture, the cruelty of it. All the pieces fit. "We're in Hell, and they want us to lose every last bit of our souls. That's what this is. We can't let them. We can't make a sacrifice. This is wrong. We have to work together. Fight them somehow."

A tall man with arms as round as my head lurched forward and grabbed my forearm in a painful grip. "You want to talk so much? You go in!"

"No!" I shouted, digging my heels in as his iron grip tightened on my arm, and he began dragging me to the door. To my horror, nobody moved to stop him. The girl in the pink fuzzy sweater cast her eyes down and chewed her nails, but did nothing more. Instead, she took a half step towards the exit door.

In a panic, I kicked and screamed, begging for anyone to intervene.

My fellow humans.

A higher power.

Anyone and anything to save me from the *Mine* door where that cheerful, deadly voice waited. As I passed, I tried to catch people's eyes, to implore them to stop the madness, but only found desolate expressions or heads lowered entirely.

They didn't care if a sacrifice was made.

So long as it wasn't them.

Pure rage blazed through me.

By now, the man needed to wrap his arms around my waist and lift me off the ground to pull me along. Throwing my head back in desperation, I heard a distinct crack as my skull connected with his face. He cried out and let go involuntarily. Pain shot through my knees as I fell to the ground. But I was on my feet a moment later, launching forward to ram my shoulder into his diaphragm like Tom had taught me for self-defense. An audible whoosh of air left the tall man's lungs as he tripped, his height a disadvantage at this moment and he stumbled back—right through the sacrifice door. He fell back, thumping to the ground with a cry of surprise. The door swung shut, as though closed by an unseen hand.

I expected screaming, or the sounds of whatever thing was hidden behind the door, but only silence met my ears. The door itself looked like the standard cheap kind a motel might use. Surely sound would travel clear through it. But nothing did. Whatever was happening to the asshole who'd tried to offer me up, it was happening quietly. The thought was somehow more terrifying, and I found myself straining my ears for any sign of what was happening behind the door.

Nothing.

Only silence. I shivered and rubbed my arms, trying to dispel the goosebumps rapidly forming. That had almost been me. Would've been me if I hadn't gotten away.

Time seemed to speed and crawl by all at once as I walked the few steps to the other door. I should have felt ashamed. I should have felt sick with myself for the death of the tall man. But, honestly? I felt accomplished. I felt powerful. I felt like a survivor. The wooden *Yours* door was cool to the touch. What lay beyond? Was it the promised freedom or something more horrifying than anything we'd seen so far?

It didn't matter.

I had no choice.

I couldn't go back.

I hesitated only a moment before stepping through. Absolute darkness surrounded me. Were we back in the entrance room?

Pain ricocheted through my head as something solid made contact with crushing force. Darkness cloaked my mind as I fell, passing out before I hit the ground.

CHAPTER 7

Embers of excitement kindled in my gut as I stepped on to the stage. In the center, The Devil himself sat upon a throne of chiseled bones, intricately connected and swirling with an aura of vengeful souls. Usually, it was me sitting there, but today my King took his rightful place. The only thing missing was me perched on his lap. His dark eyes met mine as he tapped long, sharp nails on the armrest, the sound hollow and rhythmic.

The red and white tent around us stood high. A chandelier of skulls and wax with dozens of little flames burning on the three tiers hung in the center. Below it, a dozen rows of seats filled the space. In each of them, a doomed human squirmed, and my favorite little kitten was smack in the middle. Her ears had fallen off at some point, but the black on her nose and the drawn-on whiskers remained. A few tear streaks cut the whiskers into segments—a tribute to the trauma she had experienced. Big brown eyes stared around her in shock.

I relished the fear radiating from them.

Whimpers filled the air. Such a wonderful sound. Pressing my thighs together, I worked to control the slick dripping down my leg. Damn, this turned me on. Part of me wanted to climb on The Devil and ride him right here in front of these fortunate souls. I would stare into Kitten's eyes as my breasts bounced free of the leather. Watch the way her cheeks flushed as she fought between terrified and turned on.

If only he'd let me. One glance in his direction and the arch of his brow revealed his impatience. Grinning, I faced the crowd.

"*Hell*-o, everyone," I said, chuckling at the wordplay. Everything had gone perfectly. "It's nice to see so many of you could make it to my show tonight. *You* are the lucky ones. The ones who will grace the walls of our King's private wine collection. What a privilege to please The Devil himself instead of becoming fodder for our ghouls."

Stepping to the side, I motioned towards the throne. The Devil grinned, brandishing his sharp teeth and nodding along.

The sigils I'd carved into each chair silenced their cries. But oh, how their fear permeated the air. Absolutely delicious. My mouth watered. Perhaps my King would share some of the spoils with me.

With a flick of my wrist, I signaled for one of the guests to be brought forth. Claunid stepped forward to grab a young man on the end seat. As soon as he was up off the chair, the sigil's effect ended. Immediately, he began to beg for mercy. Claunid dragged the unwilling soul to his place on stage. Deep, fresh lines engraved into the dark wood flooring made a beautiful and intricate design. One meant to hold a human in place and help the essence of their soul flow from them to The Devil. With a twisted smile that strained his stitches, Claunid shoved the human roughly onto the sigil where he remained on his knees, looking up to the Devil casually radiating a power that could crush this world beneath his hooved feet. Absolute terror contorted the man's face, making him smell all the more appealing.

The Devil leaned forward, taking a moment to examine the man.

"Please, God, no," the human mouthed.

The Devil sighed. "God has very little to do with this. Far too many needy humans calling upon Him, you see. No time for Him to save all of you."

"My King, this one is fruit-forward and full-bodied. I will age him in an oak barrel to bring out the natural earthiness of his soul. I am considering adding the flavoring of chocolate or cherry but will wait for you to let me know your preference after the tasting."

With a grunt, The Devil reached out and wrapped his large hand around the man's bottom jaw, pulling his face close to his. Once they were inches apart, The Devil flexed his hand, easily prying the human's jaws apart despite the man's struggles. The Devil's forked tongue slipped between the sharp teeth of his smile and down the throat of the whimpering man. Once it was inside his mouth, the man's eyes widened. The Devil's tongue glowed as it solidified their connection, and he tasted the man's soul. The Devil's eyes matched the intensity, their obsidian shine morphing to a red glow mirrored in the human's eyes. With a satisfied hum, The Devil released his grip on the man, allowing him to crumple to the floor, breathing hard and clutching his chest.

The Devil licked his lips and nodded.

"His flavor is acceptable. More suffering is needed to tone down the sweetness. He should have a limb removed slowly before extraction." The Devil's brow puckered as he thought it through. "Make it three hours before the limb is fully detached. As for the flavoring, I think almonds would pair nicely."

My chin dropped forward in a bow.

With a gesture from me, Claunid stepped forward to pick up the man and toss him over his broad shoulder. Another demon, this one short and round with a white face covered in staples dripping with blood, grabbed the next human. The middle-aged man unleashed a relentless string of insults as he fought each step, but once he was on his knees in front of my King, the sigil silenced his anger. The Devil didn't hesitate to take what he wanted, pressing his hand into the man's jowls and easily popping his jaw open with a snap that made it clear something had broken inside. After the tasting, The Devil turned to me, and I cowered before the fury in his still-glowing eyes.

"This one is weak at best, Isra. A murderer? What human garbage have you dared to present me with?"

Frightened, I licked at my lips frantically. All signs had pointed to a medium-bodied selection that would be spectacular with the right flavor combination. We'd investigated everyone before delivering their flyers. Sure, the man's wife had died two years ago, but it was supposed to have been from natural causes. I'd hoped his grief would give him depth. If he was a murderer, he must've killed her and made it resemble organ failure. How was I to know the man had committed murder and embittered his soul like all the others in Hell?

"I apologize, my King. Please, there are more."

The Devil's mouth twisted. His eyes promised pain for my mistake, and I caught my breath.

With a quick gesture, Claunid stepped forward, shooting me a look as he went to retrieve the murderer still on his knees before my King. With a nod, I let him know the man was to be given over to the eager ghouls behind the scenes. They were allowed precious few living humans, and I longed to be present when the little ones swarmed him like a school of piranhas, chewing and consuming until there was nothing left.

This continued for half a dozen more people. I badly wanted to present the kitten to my King, but she would go last. Oh, how I couldn't wait to see her reaction. Would she fight? Beg? Offer a trade? By the way her eyes darted around the tent, it seemed as though she searched for an escape route. Unfortunately for her, there were none.

Kitten

Of all the sights I'd seen this night, the thing sitting on its macabre throne was the worst. Black horns shining in the dim light, the she-demon called it The Devil. He was all things wicked and cruel. The spider, the centipede, the horrible monster who had flayed a living man. They were nothing next to the thing, tasting humans and coldly prescribing ways to mutilate and torture them. And for what?

As much as I wished the screams from tonight had deafened me, so I didn't have to hear the deep timbre of his voice, I heard *everything*.

We were nothing to him, and he sought to improve our flavors before consuming us. Cold sweat forced a shiver down my arms despite the heat of the room.

I would die tonight, or maybe I'd died the moment my blood touched that cursed contract, but perhaps there was still a way to win.

With no time to spare, I tried to free my hands, but they were glued to the arms of the chair by an invisible force. Just when I thought I was able to lift my pinky a fraction of an inch, someone grabbed me under my arms. Hauled to my feet, the chair released its magic, but any hope of a rescuer was dashed when I saw who held me.

It was the clown with his patchwork face of horrors, and by his grin, he was no savior.

Despair washed over me as he pulled me forward, his thick fingers digging into my arm hard enough to leave bruises.

My familiar bulky camera hung from his neck, bouncing and bumping as he dragged me closer to The Devil. Seeing it sparked a new wave of energy, one that had me attempting to elbow his ribs and slip free from his grasp.

"That's mine," I snapped, trying to grab the strap where he'd tied the lanyard back together. His throaty chuckle was the only response he gave as we reached the stage, ever closer to The Devil.

The air grew stiflingly hot as I was pulled towards the lord of Hell, and I realized the oppressive heat in the room came from him, not some secret heater.

He was the heat.

Pain rippled through my knees as I was slammed to the floor on the sigils and locked into place. My voice stolen, rendering my demands silent.

"Hmmm, yes, this one smells pleasing."

I shuddered, closing my eyes and trying to ignore the feeling of his forked tongue flicking against my cheek.

"She's a hero. The one who stepped forward when others cowered, who took a moral stand at the *Mine* door." The grating voice of the she-demon caused The Devil to stop his exploration temporarily, but then he was all the more eager. His slimy tongue darted out to lick the corners of my mouth. Whimpering, I tried to turn my face away, but he laughed.

An invisible hand straightened my head. I kept my eyes screwed shut, certain all it would take was to stare into The Devil's eyes and my mind would be completely lost. One look and I would succumb to the madness threatening to pull me under.

He gripped my chin roughly, and the scent of my own cooking flesh filled my nose even as I screamed into the silence consuming my voice. His tongue forced its way into my mouth, and I couldn't manage even a strangled cry as something inside of me ripped open and pulled into him. The pain was unlike anything I had experienced—a stabbing, tearing, searing sensation that went beyond what the nerves of my body could handle.

He broke from me with a satisfied grin.

"A hero. Yes, this one will do for my special collection, but she needs some refinement. She is full-bodied but—" His lips smacked together and a drop of his spittle fell onto my face, burning like acid. Still, he held me in position so I couldn't turn away, could only wait to hear what atrocities he had planned for me next. "There is a harsh finish that should be rounded out. Yes, she will make a fine addition once she's been through the next stage of our process." He turned my blistering face, his thumb stroking down my cheek, leaving a trail of agony.

"She'd do well to be placed on the hot plate. It'll give a toasty edge to her essence." His forked tongue flicked out to run along the seared flesh his stroke left behind. "She must be bloodied as well. Yes, well-bloodied to temper her fire and ensure she will go down more smoothly. Treat her to one-thousand cuts,

then to the oak barrels. No flavor additions for this one. I want to taste her."
His tongue caressed my cheek, and I flinched away from the searing of my flesh.
"What a bit of perfection she is, Isra. Your King is well pleased."

He shifted his back to me, and I gratefully fell forward onto the floor, savoring the pain of smashing my elbows into the hard tile because at least I'd been released from the fire of his hand on my face and the crushing weight of his malevolence. I coughed, surprised when the sound was audible. My knees, too, were unlocked from the stage. My mind turned to escape, but when I looked up, all I found was the clown watching me with a twinkle in his eye.

He stood a few feet away, with my camera in his hands. New scratches marred the black finish, and his grimy hands left smears where they touched. Lifting it to his face, he offered a raw, stretched grin as he clicked the button. A single flash, along with the audible shudder of the lens. Usually, the sound was cathartic, bringing a wave of serotonin. Instead, it was like a knife to the heart.

Chapter 8

Pain was my world.

The sound and smell of my own charred flesh as I slowly cooked on the aptly named hot plate, an added horror. The flat surface was big enough for two or three people to roast on, but I lay in the middle, all alone save for the she-demon whose gaze never wavered. She wouldn't miss a moment of my suffering. A ball of white-hot agony festered in the middle of my back no matter how I squirmed to move away from it. It wasn't long before I was glued to the table and my efforts ceased.

How long I lay on the metal table in the middle of the room, I didn't know, but I prayed to anything or anyone to save me. My fool self thought my prayers were answered when the she-demon walked up. But she just gave a delicate sniff and turned a hidden dial under the table.

The table grew impossibly hotter, and I tried to scream again even though my voice had long given out. But then the table beneath me cooled, and the she-demon pulled out a metal spatula she used to begin prying me free, tsking as she did so like my being fucking melted onto her table was such an inconvenience.

Eventually, she stood back with her hands on her hips, satisfied, though I knew the skin at the center of my back where the pain had been worst was firmly attached to the table.

"Pull her off and bring her along. I'm going to do this one personally." Her wicked grin filled me with a fear I hadn't realized I had the energy for. What else was there? The Devil had mentioned something about cuts, but surely, I would die soon.

The clown stepped forward at his mistress's bidding and pulled me off the table. A tearing sound met my ears, and a scream tried to rip its way out of my ruined throat but failed. I refused to look back to see how much of me I'd left behind.

Shaking uncontrollably from the pain, I would've cried if I could gather the moisture. The smell of burnt hair made me want to vomit, but something told me if I vomited on the clown, whatever was to happen next would be all the worse.

Where was he taking me? My body bounced painfully in his arms, my burned skin pure agony against his thoughtless jostles. Bloodied. Well-bloodied. Those were The Devil's words, and something about cuts. I shuddered, knowing I would die here and no longer caring if it would at least bring an end to the hideous pain they were about to inflict on me.

But I had to do this right. They wanted something from me, and if it was the last thing I would do, I would make sure they didn't get it.

My King was pleased, and it was time to prepare his prize. Humming a cruel song from the underworld about the beauty of splintered bones—how they shined, how they glistened—I followed behind Claunid as he took the girl to what would be her final destination.

The metal operating tables within were still soaked with blood from their previous occupants, and I eyed them with annoyance.

"Can we get this shit cleaned up, please? I'm about to work." It wasn't often I wielded the knife myself nowadays, but I wanted to make sure my kitten was perfectly prepared for The Devil.

I couldn't trust anyone else with her.

A girl wearing the ruins of a pink sweater was being hauled towards the extractor, and I put my hand on Claunid's arm so he would know to stop.

My kitten could use another little dose of fear.

The extraction began with a chair much like the ones from the tasting room. This one, however, was made of ancient wood, it had been used in Hell for centuries to constrict whatever unfortunate soul was being tortured. Human or not. Beside it stood The Machine, a metal monstrosity stretching almost to the ceiling with a hole in the center. It was a creation of my own that eased the extraction process and allowed us to work more efficiently.

Demir and Joden, a couple of low-level demons whose meat suits bubbled along the joints of their grotesque human forms, shoved the girl into the chair. Immediately, her arms locked into place on the armrests.

Oh, she tried to resist, screaming and fighting. We could put a sigil of silence on her, but the sound really was pleasant, and the ghouls did like to hear it while they worked.

It put everybody in a much better mood.

The bigger of the two demons, Demir, trailed one finger along her cheekbone, wiping away a tear as it fell. Then he brought it to his lips and sucked. Shuddering, his lips parted into a wicked grin, exposing jagged rows of teeth. One of the boils on his inner elbow burst at that moment, dripping puss onto her leg. She whimpered, her body shaking visibly, eyes wide with terror as the tendons along her jaw and temple strained against the stretched skin. Her tongue flailed uselessly as she begged for her life, spittle rolling down her chin.

The girl's terrified eyes darted around the room, seeking a salvation that wasn't coming. I chuckled, loving when they did that, like they expected one of God's angels to come bursting into the room just to save them. Demir stepped away, allowing Joden to take his place in front of the girl. In his hands, he held a special talisman. Something The Devil gave to me with careful instructions.

Only a handful of my demons knew of its existence, and even fewer were permitted to wield it. A chalice, carved from one piece of The Devil's horn. After it was shaped, my King had carved special sigils into it. To keep them hidden, and his soul magic secret, he covered it in layers of metal sourced from demon blood. I don't know how many of my kind were sacrificed for its creation, but the beautifully crude tool allowed me to continue my mission.

Joden brought the chalice to the gap in the center of my machine, carefully placing it inside before returning to the terrified girl. The chalice would draw on The Devil's own magic to activate the machine. It was beautiful.

With a yank, Joden brought over a stand holding black tubing we'd harvested from a vacuum cleaner. The tube was positioned in front of the girl and a metal head piece lowered over her head. The girl tried to turn away, and I chuckled. She must feel the way her muscles were locked into place, but she still tried. It was adorable when humans did that. The metal piece was fit over her head and a round circle with hooks was dropped in front. She watched in horror as Joden pried her mouth open and fit the metal circle behind her teeth, holding her mouth open. Joden went to press the switch, but I stepped in front.

"I've got this one, Jodie." With a wink back at Kitten, I skipped forward and pressed the red button, feeling a thrill when the machine roared to life. The chalice changed from metallic to a deep purple as the ethereal magic worked and the tube quaked with the force of suction. The girl's screams became garbled as a shimmering, translucent mist plumed from her throat and flowed out and into the dark tube. By the time it was processed and pulled into the chalice, her essence had turned a pleasing amber hue.

The girl's eyes rolled back as the talisman pulled out every last drop of her soul, the convulsions coming to a stop only once the glimmering liquid touched the brim. Joden hummed cheerfully. I walked around the dead girl, holding out my hand expectantly. Without hesitation, he pulled the chalice from the machine and handed it over. I took a sniff to get an idea for the final step of the process before wordlessly handing it to the ghoul who shadowed me.

"Put it in the barrels with a bit of cinnamon and cherries. It's not quite special collection material, but it can go into the general stores." I just hoped the others proved better than this one. My gaze fell on the kitten, who watched the dead girl with horror.

Yes, yes, she was dead now. Boo-freaking-hoo. With a roll of my eyes, I turned to the mid-level demon awaiting my command. Her tattered clothes didn't quite hide the proud horns atop her head.

"Dispose of it." If only I could use her corpse for the ghouls, but with her soul so completely extracted, they would balk at the empty flesh.

The cup's efficiency was a bit of a problem that way. With so many ghouls to feed, it'd be helpful to use all these corpses, but no. I'd have to take them out to the rural village I'd noticed nearby, let them feast and then set a fire to burn the evidence.

They'd be happy with that, but for now, I directed Claunid to bring my kitten to the blood-soaked table. I'd have preferred it was clean, but whatever. I was about to make it a whole lot bloodier, and I couldn't wait to get started.

Kitten

Everything the girl with the bad makeup and pink sweater had been, every word, every deed, bottled like it was nothing. She was left a husk, drained but rigid and not even able to slump forward. Her skin rapidly grayed. I couldn't tear my horrified gaze from her stiff form, even as the big, puss-covered demon stepped forward to rip her from her prison. Only then did she flop like a rag doll in his monstrous arms. What did they do to her? Try as I might, I couldn't recall the punishment The Devil had prescribed for her. The memories were muddled by terror and the agony that had followed.

That ripping I'd felt when The Devil tasted me, though, I remembered that well.

It had been my soul.

Confident I would die and that would be the end of it, I stared at the dead girl flung haphazardly over the demon's shoulder, and I understood.

Death was just the beginning.

They were going to prepare Bad Makeup's soul now, I realized, as the smaller creature took the crude cup back and moved to the side of the room. He poured the same shimmering liquid—the soul—into an oak barrel.

Prepare it for him. A shudder moved across my shoulders, cracking the crispy skin. I couldn't let that happen to me.

Burnt and mutilated, the she-demon didn't find me a threat at all. To be fair, I probably wasn't to her, and I would use that to my advantage. Every movement hurt, from the jarring steps as they carried me to every maneuver of my own as I brought my hands together to rub the metal charm bracelet. At least with it on, I didn't feel so alone. Mallory was with me in some way. Through the despair, tears wouldn't come. There were none. No moisture left in my body after sweating and cooking on the hot plate.

A thick band made up half the diameter of the charm bracelet, with the other half being large chain links, every one with a charm. As I held it tighter, it slipped apart. Broken and fragile from the heat. I'd have cried if I'd been able to. Mallory's bracelet breaking felt like a new slice to my broken heart.

But then I looked, and my heart stopped. Silver glinted in the light. Turning my wrist slightly, I realized the metal band held a small, curved knife.

The beach is where I feel safe.

Safe.

Of course. Mallory's words echoed in my ears as I stared in wonder at the hidden blade.

She'd kept a weapon for self-defense. Only a couple of inches long, it would do very little to my demonic attackers, but if the edges were as sharp as they looked, it would be perfect for me.

I tightened my grip on the knife, comforted by the pain as the sharp edge cut into my skin.

Not yet.

Thankfully, the bracelet slid closed without a sound. I tightened my grip on it.

It wasn't time yet.

But soon.

The clown threw me down roughly on a table slick with blood, and I felt my limbs snap into position, much as they had in the chairs. Even my head was locked straight. All I could move were my eyes, and, thankfully, my fingers.

I'd get my chance.

I just needed to be patient.

But I almost lost my nerve when the she-demon stood over me with a wicked-looking, black-handled blade and a smile that showed off her sharp teeth.

"Hey there. I know we haven't officially met, but I've been watching you, and I want to thank you in person for being awesome." She gave a shrug of one slender shoulder. The woman-thing would have been a stunner if I didn't know she was the one in charge of this house of horrors. "I mean, I couldn't have impressed him without you, really. So, thanks."

If my mouth hadn't been so dry, I would've spit in her face, but all I could manage was a feeble glare I was certain lacked any real heat.

Her blade flashed and sliced across my abdomen, cutting through the pleather that had melted to my skin, becoming one with my charred flesh. I ground my teeth against the pain. The Devil had said one thousand cuts.

This bitch was just getting started.

"Although," she sighed. "I must admit, destroying your beautiful body hurts me far more than this all hurts you. I would have preferred to destroy you in a more fun way, although it would have been just as delicious in the end, I'm sure. For both of us."

Flash, slice.

Flash, slice. She focused on my arm for a while, shallow cuts up and down it like she was making some kind of gruesome pattern. The she-demon certainly looked like she was creating art. There was a fervor in her movements and a frenetic energy in her eyes.

Occasionally, she paused to rub her clit through her skirt with one bloodied hand, clearly enjoying herself.

Flash, slice.

At some point, the pain all blended into one agonizing cacophony of torture. No longer did each individual affliction matter. Only constant torment existed between us. I was properly bloodied now, maybe even *well-bloodied*. I thought of the Devil sipping at my soul and of it disappearing into the depths of his hideous body.

No.

I wouldn't allow it.

The she-demon was desperate to craft me into the perfect beverage. She needed this. Needed me alive to put me in that machine.

When the she-demon turned her attention to my legs, I waited for a heartbeat. The chain would clang against the table when I pulled the knife open. The she-demon cut my calf, admiring the way the blackened skin cracked under pressure. I let out a guttural scream, my parched esophagus burning from the effort. The pain and strong-willed determination gave me the strength to fight the magic holding me in place. I opened the knife and let out a garbled sound to mask the noise. Thankfully, the she-demon remained focused on her incisions. My whimpers were commonplace, and the self-inflicted ones went unnoticed as I fought against the restraint and dug my tiny blade vertically along one wrist, pressing as deeply as I could and slicing through the veins. I only hoped that between the burning and blood loss, one wrist would be enough to kill me.

It hurt, but the maniacal laughter of the she-demon as she continued to slice up my body was distraction enough. Before long, my hand went numb and I could feel the warmth of my blood pooling around the deep wound, adding to the crimson blanket which encompassed me.

The pain the she-demon inflicted started to fade, and I barely reacted as the clown finally lifted my body and brought me over to the soul-sucking chair. With the last of my strength, I held the bracelet in the palm of my hand, desperate to join Mallory and hoping it would bring me nearer to her in the end, so I could apologize for being such a shitty protector and thank her for the gift of her knife.

My body was heavy, and I gave a weak smile as the demon magic locked me in place, and I felt the metaphorical invisible hand pull open my jaw.

Fuck you, I thought as I felt myself lift away from my body before the chalice could be placed against my mouth. I floated above, watching as the she-demon took the chalice and pressed it to the lips of my corpse. I may have had to leave my body behind, but my soul was safe.

Only, as I started to rise slowly upward, the chalice deepened to the same purple color which highlighted The Devil's skin. It tugged at me, a suction I couldn't quite escape from. Much to my horror, I began moving back down, the power too strong for the force drawing me gently upward.

Tears I shouldn't be able to feel streamed down my face as I reached upwards, clawing at the air as though I could grip it and use it to pull me away from the terrible fate awaiting me below.

Screaming, I watched helplessly as my feet became transparent, drifting towards the chalice and the black hole within.

Sobbing, I began to disappear into the abyss, that horrible tearing, searing pain taking over as despair squeezed my heart.

No, no, no. How could this happen now? I was so close. I'd done it. I'd tricked them all and killed myself before they could take me. Only, I'd taken my life too late, and now I would soon be packed into an oak barrel and prepared for The Devil.

Crying, I gave into the despair, resigned to my fate, when a strong hand wrapped around my wrist and pulled me upwards, easily breaking the suction that had been dragging me downward. Incredulous, I looked up, but light consumed my vision. Then I was drawn into a warm, comforting embrace. Grateful, I sank into my savior's arms.

"Welcome home, Lisa." The voice was pure sweetness and joy, happiness and truth, like this being had been waiting for me.

It was almost *heavenly*.

No.

No, no, no no no. I stared in shock as the talisman failed to extract a soul from my kitten.

Every pierce of my blade had been shallow, artful. I was a master of the craft. I'd taught fucking lessons on ensuring not to kill the victim. Death was seldom the goal, and now?

I stepped forward to examine my kitten, feeling for a pulse in her neck and taking a stumbling step back when I couldn't find one.

But what happened? *How* did this happen? Blood pooled around Kitten's hand, and I angrily snatched it up, examining the deep, jagged cut on her wrist. I hadn't done that, which meant—her fingers relaxed, and a charm bracelet clattered to the floor. No, not just a charm bracelet. A tiny, concealed weapon.

"You stupid, selfish, girl!" I roared, kicking at the corpse in front of me.

Screaming, I pulled her free of the chair and shook her.

Screwed. I was screwed. The Devil had tasted her. He wanted her, and now...I stared at her peaceful face, hating it.

What the fuck was I going to serve him tonight?

Chapter 9

The soul I'd prepared in place of my kitten's was pure, but sweet and lacking her fire. This one was no brave human ready to stick to her morals and place herself in harm's way for others, but none of them had been. I could only hope the extra time I'd given this one on the hot plate would add enough smokiness to disguise the taste.

A delicate sniff of the unstoppered bottle tottering on my red velvet-lined tray made me think I just might pull this off. The smokey scent was strong, but would it be enough? I would much rather take a reprimand for spoiling Kitten's flavor with a bit too much time on the hot plate than have him discover I'd switched her for another. With a deep breath, I walked down the short hallway, pleased with the confident way my heels tapped against the stone, and approached the mahogany double doors leading to The Devil's home away from Hell.

The doors opened with a painfully loud creak that must have drawn his attention, and sure enough, I found him lounging on the four-poster bed that dominated the room, gaze already on me. Carved from dark wood, the frame contrasted well against the tent canvas around us. A table of matching material sat against the opposite side, and I placed the tray holding the precious liquid there, hoping to buy some time before my King demanded his taste. One skull-shaped crystal glass glistened beside the elegant bottle, waiting to be filled.

Knowing my gaze couldn't linger too long on the bottle or he would suspect something, I turned to face The Devil. He sat against the headboard, his chest bare, one muscular arm resting on a fur-covered knee. His other leg stretched out, the smooth black hoof reflecting the amber light from the candles lit around the room. He tilted his head, the imposing set of horns perfectly accentuating his sharp face. Those eyes. The way they studied me made my pulse quicken.

"Isra." I loved the way his lips moved when he said my name.

"Yes, my King?"

"Crawl to me," he ordered.

Without hesitation, I dropped to my knees. My leather skirt was intentionally short today, and it did its job raising to reveal my ass and dripping cunt. Hopefully, he'd take advantage of the easy access at some point. Knowing my place, I kept my eyes low, determined not to disappoint him. The weight of his gaze grew heavier as I neared the bed.

"Stand."

With a shudder of excitement, I did so.

"Get on the bed."

The mattress dipped as I climbed on.

Instead of speaking, he curled a finger in silent order. I crawled over him, coming to a stop when his finger did. He reached out and grabbed my hair, using it to guide my back against the mattress so he could cage me beneath his broad chest. He tightened his grip on my hair to the point strands popped free. He craned my neck, tilting his head to trail his seductive tongue over the sensitive skin there, leaving behind a trail of pain and pleasure. Closing my eyes, I savored the warm sensation and clenched my thighs together. His tongue feathered the pulse. His free hand parted my legs, his nails dimpling the flesh there.

Releasing my hair, he moved his hand to my throat, easily taking hold. A reminder that I belonged to him, and he had absolute control over me. As thrilling as it was terrifying, there was electricity between us tonight. Something that felt alive around us. My senses were in overdrive as I anticipated his next move.

His tongue traced my cleavage, only stopping when he paused to pull my corset down, freeing one breast. Maybe tonight he'd undress me all the way. It wasn't often he viewed me completely naked, but when he did, I savored every second his eyes roamed my flesh. His sharp teeth bit into my cleavage, soliciting a moan. Only after tasting the blood did he move down to my spread legs. His hot tongue traced my core before pushing inside for a taste. Then he pulled out enough to curl around my clit.

When I squirmed, his fingers tightened around my throat. Just enough to prove his absolute control over me. I gripped the sheets, struggling to hold still as he began to work me. A fire grew between my legs, and he fanned those flames with his mouth.

The Devil devoured me in all the right ways, his teeth catching the skin occasionally when I squirmed too much. All too soon, my muscles clenched, and I cried out, holding the sheets tighter. I wanted to grab his horns in a desperate attempt to keep him between my thighs longer, but I knew better. Thankfully, he sucked on my clit, prolonging the intense waves of pleasure for a few tantalizing moments. In one swift movement, he repositioned, holding me in place as he pressed the tip of his cock against my pussy. He entered quickly, filling me with every inch and stretching me.

This moment wasn't for me, though, and he made that clear as he thrust at an impossible pace. Giving me no time to catch my breath as he worked towards his climax. Pleasure glinted in his glowing red eyes. It thrilled me, knowing I could provide this for him. All of this, everything I did, was for him.

"My King." I moaned. It took everything I had not to reach for him. I wanted to dig my nails into his back as he slammed into me. His body tensed. The sound of slickness between us increased as his hot seed filled me. Just knowing I made him cum brought another orgasm, and I rode the wave gratefully. Until, all at once, The Devil released my throat and rolled off me to sit against the pillows once more.

I lay there, working to catch my breath as he got comfortable.

"Bring me the essence, Isra." A simple order. One that my body protested as I pushed off the bed to walk to the table on shaky legs. I could only hope he thought my trembling was solely due to my body reeling from our encounter. With a deep breath, I picked up the tray and carried it to the bed. His seed dripped down my leg. Setting the tray on the mattress, I opened the bottle and poured the drink into the glass. He took it, holding it up with scrutiny. He swirled it, watching closely as it shimmered in the candlelight. Every second of examination chased the pleasure away, replacing it with fear and anticipation.

He inhaled the aroma, taking a sip and moving it around his mouth before swallowing. He held my gaze as he took another.

"Isra."

Dropping to my knees beside the bed, I said, "Yes, my King?"

When he extended his arm with an open palm, I crawled forward to rest my cheek against it.

"I just have one question for you." He smiled, and I relaxed into his palm, awaiting his praise.

"What is it, my King?" I pressed myself against him like a feline in heat, already craving more of him.

"Did you really think you could fool me?"

"Hmm?" Opening my groggy eyes, I made to lift my head, but his fingers curled around one of my horns, holding me in place.

"You heard me."

Swallowing, I tried to plaster a look of innocence on my face. "I don't know what you mean. This is the girl you tasted, my King. The kitten." I hated how my tone rose at the end, as did my heart rate. Something sparkled in his eye. I wanted to believe it was approval or humor, and maybe it was, but not for the reasons I hoped.

"It's not and you are in an awful lot of trouble."

Fire flashed in his red-rimmed eyes. Pain ripped through my neck as he wrenched my head to the side. I fought back the panic in my gut. I messed up, sure, but maybe I could talk my way out of it. Certainly, I'd been too useful to just get rid of, right? Didn't this carnival prove that?

"My King—"

"Silence." In one word, he stole the voice from my throat and the air from my lungs.

With a gasp, I reached up to rub my neck reflexively, trying to coax the muscles to work again.

"You dare to try and hide the one I chose from me? Maybe you took her for yourself, hm?"

When my apology came as a garbled gasp for breath, he leaned closer, tilting his head to bring one ear near my lips even as he gripped my hair harder. "Hmm? What are you saying?"

Remaining calm, I tried to silently ask him to release me. He *tsk*ed, his forked tongue slipping between red lips. "When did you become such a festering pustule of disappointment?"

His words cut like a knife. All I'd ever done was try to please him. Were all those years truly meaningless?

While he continued to hold me with one arm, his other took hold of my chin and wrenched my jaw open.

Surely, he wouldn't. Would he?

Could he?

I was a demon. Our souls were an inferior sort, bitter and gritty on the tongue, but there was a certainty in his eyes as his forked tongue flickered into my mouth.

I couldn't look away from his evil eyes. I shoved at his chest, trying desperately to push him away, but it was like moving a boulder. As a demon, my strength was enough to crush humans, but I was nothing compared to the King of Hell. To him, I was little more than an insignificant bug.

With all my strength, I fought against him, but he didn't flinch in the least, his grip unrelenting.

A crimson light swirled in his eyes as he stared back at me.

My light.

Self-preservation became my only concern, but fighting was pointless. My vision blurred, white and red fighting for dominance as searing pain exploded like fireworks in my mind. My strength faded until every muscle went limp. Shadows ebbed in the corners of my vision, tendrils of darkness growing until there was nothing left.

Icy cold seeped into my bones, weighing them down as every particle that was once me tumbled into the darkness of my King.

THE DEVIL

"Really, Isra, you shouldn't have tried to fool the King of Trickery." Of course, I knew what had happened to the soul of my prize, but I'd waited to see how Isra would deal with the situation.

My mouth was still dry and there had been an unpleasant graininess to Isra's soul that spoke of her quest for power, but my underlings needed the occasional lesson and Isra's attempts at deception could not go unpunished. With a grumble, I used my long black nails to pick a piece of something out of my incisor and examined it.

A blackened crumb wriggled pitifully on the edge of my nail, and I laughed as it fought to escape with all its might.

"Are you still trying to get away, Isra?" With a low growl, I licked the last bit of her soul up, reveling in her scream as I sucked her to the back of my mouth and swallowed hard. Casting her down to the endless darkness of my stomach where her being would slowly be broken down and consumed over the next two thousand years.

A presence hovered by the door.

"You, there." My booming voice echoed in the cavernous room. "What is your name?"

A bold one to come so close without being summoned.

But I did like a bit of boldness in my generals.

"It is I, my King, Ta–Ta–Talsine." Her fear was palpable.

I eyed the demon. The flesh she wore was a deep red. Only demons of high caste could influence a body that way, but the clothes she wore over her skeletal frame were torn and ratty.

How much of Isra's demise had she watched?

Standing, I walked slowly over to the demon, knowing the steadiness of my approach would heighten her fear. Her eyes remained lowered even as I stood in front of her.

With a hand firmly holding her jaw, I tilted her face up and met her eyes.

Mmm, yes. There was a fire there, and a desire to prove herself. Which meant the clothes were a front. A high demon wearing rags trying to appear lesser so others would lower their guard.

She'd do.

"What did you see, Talsine?" I waited, before watching her jaw work and realizing I held it too tightly. I released the pressure, but not my hold on her.

"I saw a traitorous beast who dared to cross her master get put down like she deserved." A note of anger danced on the edge of her otherwise flat voice.

"Good girl." I purred, flickering my tongue across her cheek to taste her essence. She stood still as I explored her face, my tongue dipping into her mouth. Talsine shuddered at the bitter taste of my venom, but she didn't pull away.

Slowly, I turned away before speaking to her over my shoulder.

"You're in charge of my carnival now, Talsine. My shelves have been re-stocked. You have one hundred years before I visit again."

"Yes, my King."

"And Talsine?"

"Yes."

My mouth was dry, the taste unpleasant.

"Bring me the soul of a child. A plump one who has never known a day of suffering. I need something sweet to wash down the demon."

"Yes, my King."

With a sigh, I waited until I heard the click of Talsine closing the double doors before stabbing at the fabric of the realm with my nail and tearing open a hole through which I could view my domain.

Between the jagged edges of reality, a flat stone pathway stretched before me. Familiar obsidian pieces, broken apart by the reddish glow of fire beneath, led into darkness. One has to step through to see the true beauty of my home. The colors were impossibly deep for this world, and I hated how muted everything looked through the window I'd created. Fire and brimstone, as the humans liked to call it, but the description did very little to represent the wicked beauty bound in chains and flame. A true reprieve from the fleshy world of Earth.

The screams of the damned soothed my irritation.

I left the portal open so I could hear them as I went to Isra's corpse and plucked out an eye. Onyx rimmed storms of red, orange, and yellow. Intelligence and a quest for glory still gleamed, even with her acidic soul no longer residing behind them, her last look frozen forever in the still-dead eyes. More than anything, I admired the way she looked up to me with absolute desire even as I'd prepared to consume her.

She did have beautiful eyes, I'd give her that, and now they belonged to me. They would look good on my mantle.

Another hundred years before I would visit this place again, and I couldn't wait to see what Talsine did with it. What new essences she would secure. What new ways she would find to please me.

This carnival really was a *hell of a thing*.

The End

About the Authors

Laurae Knight is an exceptionally talented writer, dabbling in darkness and romances with fairytale vibes and plus size baddies. She strives to be an advocate for authors and is a proud co-founder of the Sisterhood of the Black Pen. With her amazing fantasy and horror stories, readers can expect dark humor, steamy romances, and relatable yet diverse characters surviving fantastical and chaotic worlds you won't want to leave behind.

When she isn't writing, she can be found chasing monsters and ghosts with her children in the dense forest, cuddling her dogs and cat, hunting seashells on the nearby beach with her husband and mom, or taking the chance to touch something questionable.

She can be found on Facebook (Laurae Knight) or on TikTok, Instagram, and Threads (LauraeKnightWrites). Follow her to keep up with ongoing projects like Silent Sunflower, her sapphic sleeping beauty retelling.

In addition to writing horror, and organizing anthologies as a co-founder of The Sisterhood of the Black Pen, Faye also writes dark and gritty fantasy with strong romantic subplots. Her readers can expect dark themes, high stakes, soulmates, and fierce heroines who struggle through their broken pasts to find connection and salvation. Faye's works regularly feature non-human characters with entirely human feelings and weaknesses, offering her readers a compelling mix of escapism and relatable characters.

Follow Faye on tiktok (faye.knightly.writer) and instagram (@faye_knightly_writer) for updates on her writing projects.

Faye shares her writing space with a wildly supportive husband who regularly leaves her 'cofferings' (the last dredges of his coffee left out on the table for her to find), three tiny humans who provide just the right amount of distraction, and a former Egyptian street cat who warms her lap to the purrfect writing temperature.